"Asking around town for me actually got these guys all in my face. I wasn't prepared and had to come up with some type of excuse."

"What the hell are you sidestepping, Therese?" Maybe his words could have been a little less confrontational, a little less loud. *Not really.* "Dammit, I need some answers."

"The truth is I've been on this case for over three years."

Case? Three years on a *case*? "I knew it." He slowed to a stop, wanting to caress her hair, all that silkiness. "You're undercover FBI."

Her hands waved him to silence even as her lips puckered sexily again. "Shh. Don't say it aloud even if we're alone. When you started asking around town for me, I shrugged it off. But then you kept asking and it's made my boss—" she shrugged "—a little angsty."

"Angsty enough to send your, um...protection detail?" Hit men were more like it. God, he wanted to pull her to him and kiss her. He shook it off. Men. Guns. Undercover. Favor. Focus.

CRIMINAL ALLIANCE

USA TODAY Bestselling Author

ANGI MORGAN

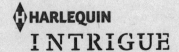
HARLEQUIN
INTRIGUE

Thanks for the years of encouraging words and support, Therese!
You deserve a great, capable heroine named after you.
Lori, Amanda and Robin...couldn't have done it without you.

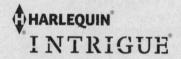

ISBN-13: 978-1-335-13638-1

Recycling programs
for this product may
not exist in your area.

Criminal Alliance

Copyright © 2020 by Angela Platt

This edition published by arrangement with Harlequin Books S.A.

For questions and comments about the quality of this book,
please contact us at CustomerService@Harlequin.com.

Harlequin Enterprises ULC
22 Adelaide St. West, 40th Floor
Toronto, Ontario M5H 4E3, Canada
www.Harlequin.com

Printed in U.S.A.

Angi Morgan writes about Texans in Texas. A *USA TODAY* and *Publishers Weekly* bestselling author, her books have been finalists for several awards, including the Booksellers' Best Award, *RT Book Reviews* Best Intrigue Series and the Daphne du Maurier Award. Angi and her husband live in North Texas. They foster Labradors and love to travel, snap pics and fix up their house. Hang out with her on Facebook at Angi Morgan Books. She loves to hear from fans at angimorganauthor.com.

Books by Angi Morgan

Harlequin Intrigue

Texas Brothers of Company B

Ranger Protector
Ranger Defender
Ranger Guardian
Criminal Alliance

Texas Rangers: Elite Troop

Bulletproof Badge
Shotgun Justice
Gunslinger
Hard Core Law

West Texas Watchmen

The Sheriff
The Cattleman
The Ranger

Texas Family Reckoning

Navy SEAL Surrender
The Renegade Rancher

Hill Country Holdup
.38 Caliber Cover-Up
Dangerous Memories
Protecting Their Child
The Marine's Last Defense

Visit the Author Profile page at Harlequin.com.

CAST OF CHARACTERS

Wade Hamilton—Lieutenant in the Texas Rangers, Company B. He trusts his gut and has a habit of acting before he thinks things through.

Therese Ortis—An undercover FBI agent working hand in hand with Homeland Security. Wade owes her a favor after saving his life, and it's time to collect.

Company B—Jack McKinnon, Heath Murray and Slate Thompson. Wade helped with their love lives; now they intend to return the favor.

Rushdan Rival—A billionaire who tried to kill Wade. He has a finger in almost every illegal pie in Dallas.

Public Exposure—A group actively promoting to use less social media. Are they real or a cover for a domestic terrorist group?

Prologue

"Dammit, Hamilton. It doesn't matter if you were right. You broke every rule we have. If it were up to me, I'd kick you to the curb like you deserve." Major Clements slapped his hand against his thigh as he paced in front of the door.

Wade Hamilton stood at attention, something he'd rarely done since becoming a Texas Ranger. Eyes straight ahead, he couldn't see his commander walking behind him. But hey, even if he stood directly in front, Wade couldn't focus on the major's expressions. His left eye was still swollen from the beating he'd taken a week ago and everything was blurry. He couldn't judge if this was the end…or just a very long reprimand.

Wade could feel Major Clements just over his right shoulder. Out of his peripheral vision, he saw the major's hand clenched in a fist, the knuckles white from the tight grip. His supervisor had been angry before.

Yeah, several times before.

But hopefully, he could remember that Wade had saved lives. Didn't that count for something? His partner had reminded him often enough that Wade trusted his gut too much. But this time Jack was grateful for it.

"It seems that I don't have a final say," the major continued. "Seems that someone at headquarters put in a good word. Who knows, maybe the woman you helped save talked with someone. Or maybe the top brass doesn't want to have to explain why a Texas Ranger from Company B was fired after saving someone from the state fire marshal's office. Hell, I have no idea."

Major Clements's boots struck the floor, paused and pivoted again.

It wasn't the first time the major had given him a lecture. It *was* the first time he hadn't been looking at Wade when he delivered it. No matter the words about how lucky he was and unknown friends at headquarters, Wade still wasn't too sure about job security.

"I drew the line at the suggestion you be given a commendation. Rule breakers should not be rewarded. The example you've set is not a good one. I'm very disappointed in you, Lieutenant." The major's voice was tempered with sadness instead of anger.

"I understand, sir."

"Good." He walked back to his desk, putting both fists knuckle down on the polished wood and leaning toward Wade. "And yet, I don't hear an apology or simple words like *it won't happen again*."

"That goes without saying, sir."

"Do you really believe that, Wade? I hope you'll at least try not to play the hero. You barely survived this time. But since I can't fire you, in order to rein you in a bit…" He sat. A good sign that Wade hadn't lost his job. "You're benched."

"Excuse me, sir?" Wade's eyes moved to make contact with the major. One stern look was enough to have him back at attention. "I'm not sure I understand."

"Desk duty, Lieutenant. You'll report here every day. And every day there will be files for you to work on. You are not to leave this office from the hours of nine to five. I don't want to hear about you even going for lunch. You got me?"

"Loud and clear, sir."

"Dismissed."

"But what about the case, sir?" Wade looked just above the major's head, concentrating on keeping his eyes from pleading with the man in charge of his fate. "We only touched the surface of what crimes Rushdan Reval is behind. This is our way into that scumbag's organization."

"We've been ordered to stand down, Lieutenant. I said dismissed."

Wade left the office barely able to swallow, feeling grateful that he had a job, wondering how he'd survive sifting through files—especially paperwork that wasn't even his—and disappointed in himself that he'd been close to accessing Reval's group and had messed up...bad.

His partner, Jack MacKinnon, gave him a "what's up" look from across the room. Slate Thompson and Heath Murray, along with the other Company B Rangers, gave him a wide berth and no eye contact. They all probably thought he was heading to his desk to clean it out. No one really expected him to keep his job, his rank or his anything.

He made it to his desk, still using the crutch the hospital had forced on him. Honestly, he could barely see his chair since his left eye was killing him. It was the roll-y thing behind the big block of wood. Yeah, he could joke but not laugh—the cracked ribs were too painful.

The doctors had been straight about the headaches that wouldn't go away for a while. Even straighter about the possibility his sight might not ever be 100 percent again. Rest—sitting-down-and-not-moving kind of rest, to be more specific—was what they demanded.

They hadn't cleared him for anything. But after two days of sitting inside his house, he'd finagled his recovering body behind the wheel of his truck and driven the fifteen minutes to headquarters. It had been more painful sliding out and hitting the ground with both feet.

He sat, putting the crutch on the floor next to the wall his desk was pushed against. He heard himself suck air through his teeth as he rolled into place.

"You okay?" Jack patted him lightly on the back. "Looks like you're still employed."

Dammit, he hadn't seen Jack come up behind him. He jumped, then hissed again in pain.

"For the moment. And only at this wonderful desk." He petted it like a dog.

"Always the cutup. How long?" his partner asked before sitting on the corner of his desk.

"You got me." It hurt too much to shrug. And it hurt too much to focus across the aisle. Everything really was mostly a blur.

"Man, I'm not sure how long it'll take for him to trust you again." Jack rubbed his chin, then the back of his neck—or at least that was what it looked like through the fog. "I'm sort of surprised I'm not stuck here, too. On second thought, it was entirely your fault I was involved in the first place."

"Don't go there, man. Not only did you get to make a serious arrest because I asked for a favor, but you also got a girlfriend out of it. Who I should probably thank for saving my job with a word from her state-level boss. You can say that I'm responsible for setting you two lovebirds up."

"You could say that." Jack stood, removing his gun from his desk drawer and placing it in its holster. "But if you do, I might just have to kick your butt." He laughed. "Your desk duty explains why I'm on loan to Dallas PD for a while."

"They're still shorthanded after the loss of their officers. You'd think the major would want me out there with you."

His partner raised his eyebrows almost into his hairline. "Get real. You know I trust you with my life. But man, you got to learn to play the game. Rangers have a specific duty and—"

"And are restricted to following the law. Yeah, I know. I heard that lecture for the past hour while standing at attention. I thought the major would go harder on me if I reminded him I'm having problems standing."

Jack clapped him on the shoulder. Wade tried not to wince. He was determined to force his body to at least stay upright.

"I was going to say," Jack continued, "that we have a proud tradition. Our motto might be 'One Riot, One Ranger,' but that doesn't mean it has to be us doing things alone. I'm here for you. Always will be. No matter what."

"Thanks, Jack. It's appreciated."

"Keep your head down and fly under the radar. Don't go looking for trouble."

"I never look, man. It just always seems to find me. Watch your back since I won't be there to protect you."

"Like you did by getting beat up so bad you can't stand?"

"Three cracked ribs isn't too bad." He squinted through his good eye. "Besides, they took me by surprise."

"Right."

Wade watched his partner leave the office without

him, passing one of the clerks on his way. A clerk with a box, heading straight toward his desk.

"Major Clements said you should go through these, Wade." She dropped the box on the floor next to his chair. "You need to verify that all the appropriate reports are in order and scanned or the data inputted. Basically, that everything's ready for trial or to turn over to headquarters. When you're done, I have the rest of the alphabet waiting." She turned to leave but pivoted back to his desk. "Remember that these files need to be locked up each night."

Wade lifted the lid and pulled the folder at the end… Carla Byrnhearst. "That's just great." One box got him through two letters. He shoved the file back inside and pulled the Ader file from the other end.

Keep his head down.

Do the time at his desk.

Accept the punishment.

Keep his job.

He could do this. He'd wanted to be a Texas Ranger for too long. One man had put everything on the line to keep him from a life of crime. After that, all his focus had been toward obtaining that goal. College, Texas DPS, the highway patrol, three long years near the border and finally an opening and assignment to Company B.

These men were his brothers now. His desk phone rang and he answered.

"Hey, sexy. Just checking up on you."

Therese. Trouble did have a habit of finding him. God, just the woman's voice sent electricity shooting through his veins. Where had she been? Where was she now? Last week in the hospital, he'd forced another ranger to run Therese Ortis's name. She should have been awaiting trial for her involvement with Rushdan Reval, the Dallas crime syndicate leader who had just tried to kill him. But there had been nothing.

"I guess I owe you something—at least dinner—for saving my life." His mind was already following the steps to have the call traced.

He'd seen her once. Spoken to her fewer than half a dozen times. And he was caught, dangling at the end of her string. In fact, he'd swallowed her enticing voice and innuendos hook, line and sinker.

"Even though I'd enjoy that very much, I don't think it would help you get off desk duty," she purred.

"You're the one who kept me my job?"

"Ladies never kiss and tell, Wade." She paused long enough to let the words have their desired effect. "Gotta run, Ranger Big Man. Till next time."

"Wait…"

Too late. The line disconnected. He didn't have to inquire about the number—he knew it would be a dead end. Just like each time before. His mystery woman had a habit of swooping in for the save and disappearing until she needed him again.

He opened the file and started. With any luck, he could get through a letter each day. Twenty-six days stuck in a chair. Behind a desk. Watching his fellow rangers do the heavy lifting.

No playing hero.

Most investigating happened from a chair anyway. Sitting here would give him plenty of time to discover just what the mystery surrounding his lady was all about. Yeah, he could do this. Especially now that he was properly motivated.

And man oh man…he was definitely motivated to find Therese Ortis.

Chapter One

Just another two-for-one longneck Friday special. Wade sat on the same barstool he'd ended his nights on and had claimed for years. This particular stool was the last one next to the wall, located where no one could catch him by surprise. Only his right side was open to patrons. Better for his vision, especially now that it got fuzzy from time to time.

He should be somewhere else.

Maybe somewhere more respectable for a Texas Ranger. That wasn't here. Someplace he could share that he was a ranger. Or maybe be with his friends. But they all had girlfriends. Heath was back home with his wife. Slate might as well be married. And Jack—his so-called partner—was engaged.

He should find some other friends. Maybe some who liked to…to what? Watch a game? Play trivia over some chicken wings? It didn't matter where he went or what barstool he ended up on. He'd still be looking at every dark-haired woman who walked in the door to see if it was her.

Dammit. He couldn't keep this up. Six weeks was long enough visiting bars on lower Greenville Avenue. His search for Agent Therese Ortis needed to end.

Soon. No. Tonight. He'd shown his face once too often in other dives. Earlier the barkeeps had waved him past their place, in a hurry to get the discouraged ranger on his way. His badge was far from good for their business.

So here he sat. His go-to joint that knew him from way back. The one place where they gave him a pass for having a badge.

Twisting the rest of his lime slice into his Mexican beer, he studied the peel—more interested in the citrus than in anyone around him. He needed to take Jack's advice. If Therese wanted to get in touch… Well, she knew how. She'd done it before to save Megan and a second time to save his hide before Rushdan Reval blew him up inside a building.

Across the room, the door banged open. Heads—including his—turned toward the noise.

What the hell?

"Wade!" The woman who had haunted his dreams crossed the sixty feet, dodging drunks and other happy-hour patrons who had quickly returned to their conversations.

"You have got…" she began, too loudly, before nervously looking around and landing next to him at the bar. "You've got to stop your…your inquiries. Are you listening to me? I'm furious."

No, he hadn't been listening. Dressed in the smallest bright yellow dress—more like a piece of a dress that could still be respectful—he barely noticed anything else. The color set off her dark brown hair.

The bling around her neck drew his eyes straight to the diving-low plunge between her breasts. How the hell was she walking in those heels?

Shoot. How did the dress stay in place?

The woman who'd actually 100 percent saved his life licked her lips and drew a deep breath. Trying to ignore her, he looked down at the bar, stabbing the three lime slices with a plastic sword.

"Hey, Wade, hon?" Her erotic voice whispered close to his ear while her feathery touch on his hand shot all sorts of feelings through him.

Six weeks without a word.

And she was mad. *At him?*

Even though she'd been caught working with crooks last year, he'd never believed she was on the wrong side of the law. Something in their sparse conversations had forbidden him from thinking badly of her. Then six weeks ago he'd found out—like a kick to the head—she was working with the FBI or something. Nobody talked. Lots of secrets. Had he forgiven her for taking away a major case?

Probably not.

There was no mistake who she spoke to. She'd stopped so close her breath of air brushed his bare neck, encouraging him to act. But he wouldn't. He didn't have the right. Even if she had called him *hon*.

"I like you in a T-shirt. It shows off these strong arms. But this button-up looks great on you, too. It brings out the steel blue in your eyes."

He could tell her he liked her dress. Or not.

Yeah, she squeezed his biceps. Yeah, she puckered her lips together like she waited for a kiss.

"No."

"Are you sure?" She eased onto the stool next to him, her long legs reaching sideways under his. Damn, that yellow silky thing climbed up to her hip. "I haven't even asked anything."

Wait. Were they talking about a kiss or the favor he thought she was about to ask? He should consider himself lucky that the stools weren't close enough for him to pull her onto his lap to find out. *Lucky?*

Therese twisted away from him to face the opening door and back again with a blank look. A big fella walked inside, propping the door open with his foot and calling to a buddy on the sidewalk. They both entered, finally shutting the door to keep the cooler air in and the blistering summer heat outside.

Everything about her demeanor changed. Where she'd been full of anger she was now soft. She closed her eyes, drawing a deep breath through her nose and making her breasts swell in the tight dress. Then she wet her lip gloss with the tip of her tongue. To stop his drool, he tipped the beer to his mouth, drinking her in with his eyes.

The fresh burst of lime made him lick his lips, or

was he mirroring the seductress beside him? Then her dark red lips parted ever so slowly. Slower than necessary and very practiced. Hell, he could give in right then, doing whatever she asked, having no idea what it might be.

Instead he broke off his stare and looked around the intimate, off-the-beaten-path bar. Mostly regulars with the exception of the last two men. Every corner was shadowed and filled with secrets, but he didn't butt his nose in. He knew the ins and outs. Knew what to expect. He'd been coming here since college and it didn't hurt that no one broadcast that he was a Texas Ranger. He'd never had a need to show his badge. Not here.

"I know it's been a while since I've called. Please don't be annoyed with me." She swiveled on the stool, reaching for his limes, daring him not to look down the low-cut dress she flashed under his chin.

"I'd have to care to be angry. Or annoyed," he lied. He didn't know the reason for her personality switch, but he'd play along.

"There's just been a lot going on, hon—" She pouted.

Pouted? Therese Ortis didn't seem the pouting kind.

What the hell was going on? She knew he'd been looking for her and seemed pretty doggone upset about it less than five minutes ago.

"So you aren't angry, annoyed or even a little hurt, baby?" she smiled with a knowing smile, circling a deep red nail around the back of his hand.

Hon? Baby? What was she trying to pull? She reached out, taking his extra lime and swiping her tongue across it. She knew exactly how to make *him* nervous. But she was the one shaking like a leaf in a windstorm—the only thing that kept him from showing her just how angry he wasn't.

Yeah, he was succumbing to the seductress line. What man wouldn't? But it was the trembling that got him.

Her eyes darted in every direction, checking for trouble. The bartender walked to the other end of the room and she leaned in close.

"I need a big favor. I can explain everything if you give me a chance."

Even though the intensity changed from flirtatious to urgent, he still answered, "I'm all out."

Explain? Nice fantasy. Therese never explained. He poured more than a sip of beer down his throat. He tipped the bottle toward her, politely asking if she wanted something. She shook her head while he caught the bartender's eye and ordered two more.

"I promise not to land you on desk duty again. What do you say?" she asked in a low, sensual voice he had fallen prey to a few times already.

Wade had wanted to connect with her for over a year. Why the hesitation? *Desk duty. Uncertainty. Tired of being used. Downright irritation at being ignored.*

"I say—" he grinned way too big "—that you haven't mentioned anything I haven't heard before."

"I'm sure that can't be true," she still whispered.

"Considering I can recall all seven conversations we've ever had… Yeah, I'm pretty sure I can clearly remember every word that you've said." *And exactly what you haven't.*

"I really, really think you're going to be interested in my favor, hon."

"Nope." He kept his voice low, matching hers.

He was done. Had nothing left. Finished. Kaput. Refused to get involved. *Remember?* And yet, completely curious.

"Is there anything I could do or say to change your mind?" She drew circles on his shoulder, dragging her long fingernail down his arm until she got to his hand.

She looked innocent. If he knew her better he might think she seemed desperate. But he didn't know her better. She came to him when she needed something. Case or no case, he didn't like being used.

And he hated giving in to her, to anybody.

Therese's eyes darted to the mirror.

The two large men moved away from the opposite end of the bar and Therese stiffened. Obvious to him since she held his hand. Probably not obvious to the men who had eyes for no one else in the room. They looked like typical guys, with the exception of the bulges under their jackets. Jackets worn for the simple reason of hiding the weapons.

They were there for her—obviously.

"Wade," she said way too loudly. "I'm so hungry."

"What?"

She dropped a finger across his lips to stop his

next question. Her eyes moved to the mirror. His hand gently tugged hers from his face back to the bar and slid a longneck bottle into it.

"I guess I need to hear about that favor after all." He squeezed a lime slice and pushed it through the neck of the sweating bottle.

Chapter Two

Normally, Therese wouldn't have paid any attention to someone as good-looking as Texas Ranger Wade Hamilton. He was almost too good-looking.

Dark brown hair swooped back off his forehead. Dark blue eyes framed by masculine-shaped brows. And a sprinkle of chest hair. Just visible tonight with the open collar in his Texas-blue dress shirt. She'd seen the outline of that chest in a T-shirt a couple of times, too. Just like she'd admitted a few minutes ago.

Oh, yeah, she'd kept up with him. Back when she was in control. Right up to coming face-to-face with him at a crime scene six weeks ago.

She should have gone to him covertly and explained what she was doing. Wade would have left things alone then. When she'd told her handler her plan, he'd laughed and ordered her to stay clear of the ranger. Everyone had seen what they called "smoldering looks" from Wade. And they'd made it known they'd seen right through her attempt to act immune.

So she'd avoided the tall, handsome ranger and paid off the bars where he kept asking after her. But the damage was done. Wade had shown his badge one too many times. Rushdan was convinced she'd sold him out to the cops.

Of course she had. But he'd had no clue before Wade Hamilton kept asking everywhere for her.

The moment she'd seen Wade sitting on that very barstool last year she'd lost her breath. When he hadn't recognized her cowering in the corner, she'd just watched. She hadn't stopped thinking about him since that Friday night.

The very first time they'd met, he'd literally swept her off her feet while rescuing her teenage version. When he hadn't recognized her as an adult, it had stung a little, but it was totally understandable. A lot had gone down that night. And wouldn't you know it, now he was the only man she could trust to keep her alive.

Being alone would get her killed. Period.

If only she could wait or fill him in on why she needed him. Crossing her fingers that he'd be sitting on his barstool, she'd come here looking for him. Unlike how she'd avoided it every Friday night since she'd returned to Dallas. She'd been ordered not to speak to him or meet him under any circumstances.

Her last conversation with Rushdan had left her uncomfortable. He did the hinting thing, talking around her to only the men, asking why a certain Texas Ranger was asking all over Dallas for her.

When she'd left the offices, the two thugs behind her had followed.

Okay, she felt desperate and her brain began to panic a little. Pretty sure those men had been sent to take her out. Three years of undercover work shot because she'd been ordered not to talk to the man beside her. Yeah, panic closed in, making the bar feel even smaller.

With one eye on the bar mirror, she watched Rushdan's men loitering just inside the bar's door. She pushed her nerves aside and daringly placed her palm on Wade's thick-muscled thigh. He actually jumped a little. How sweet.

"This seat taken?" Rushdan's head hit man knew it wasn't. He knew she'd come in alone. And knew she didn't carry a weapon. Or at least thought he knew.

Leaning away from Wade, she tried to give the man following her a brilliant, reassuring smile. "We're on a date, sugar. Please don't try to pick me up."

Please go with it, Wade. Don't yell at me for acting like we're lovers. It is all your fault.

"As a matter of fact…we were about to leave." Wade tipped the remains of his beer between perfectly handsome lips. "We're meeting friends for dinner."

"Then you're not drinking that longneck?" Rushdan's guy slanted his body, blocking her view of the entrance. He moved so close to her as he reached for the beer she hadn't touched that she was afraid she'd slide off the stool trying to avoid him. Wade's legs connected with her body, effectively catching her. Too bad there wasn't more time to flirt. As nervous as he seemed, she could have had some fun.

"Go for it. The little lady's afraid she'll spoil her appetite." Wade stood, dropping money on the bar before sliding his hands back onto her shoulders, his body next to her back, steadying her. "You can have our stools just as soon as we go."

His gentle twang could melt her heart under different circumstances.

"We'll never make our reservation, hon. Not if you do anything…to slow us down." She licked her lips and knew they appeared sexy. She had much too much practice at flirting and yet it still made her uncomfortable.

Give her a 9mm and a target at fifty yards and she'd be completely at ease. She mentally demanded her nerves to settle. Otherwise she'd need a bucket to catch the sweat from her palms.

The dumb blonde routine—even if she was a brunette—had never been her dream assignment for undercover work. But she was stuck with it. Her carefully constructed identity called on her to be soft, vulnerable and not too smart. At least Rushdan Reval considered her soft.

Leaving the stool, she deliberately fell into the side of Reval's man, letting her hands play across his flabby chest and lifting his weapon from his holster.

Rushdan's second goon took a quick step toward them. She backed up quickly, passing the gun to Wade, who aimed straight at their assailants. The bartender jerked to a halt along with the rest of those in the bar.

"Uh-uh-uh." She waved a finger at Rushdan's hired help. "What will your friends say if they knew you lost your weapon? I won't tell if you don't."

Wade jerked her back to his side.

Damn, he's a rock. She dropped the thoughts about Wade's body and planned their walk past Rushdan's men. Wade acted like she'd been his for a decade—not two minutes. Maybe he was used to women throwing themselves at his feet, but she wasn't used to being held.

She might play the part of easy...but she hadn't had a real relationship since college. Undercover work had major pitfalls.

Her stomach did a double backflip when Wade's hands darted a little lower on her waist than she'd intended. She didn't change their direction. She needed to leave this bar and take him with her. How else could she explain her presence on lower Greenville and try to salvage three years of undercover work?

Lying to Rushdan about why Wade had been looking for her bought her time this afternoon. Time to find him. Granted, it had been spur of the moment and she'd been unable to contact her team for backup. But something—or someone—had made

Rushdan suspicious. When the crime boss sent these guys to follow her, it was for one reason...elimination.

She began the longest walk of her career. Wade's long fingers slid over her hip and back up around her waist, distracting her with their heat. Her hands flew to fan her face—half acting and half needing to cool her hot cheeks.

Wade pulled the door open, waiting for her to go through. She wanted one last look at the men chasing her and turned. The movement brought them closer, making her aware of Wade's body, the complete maleness of him.

A sparkle in his eye caught her attention. *The jerk. He's laughing at me.* Maybe she'd been flirting a little too much and couldn't stop herself. It was as if the sensual woman in her—although scarcely unleashed—chose that very moment to take control.

She turned completely into Wade and the slinky thing the salesgirl called a dress rose higher along her thigh. His fingertips brushed the bare skin just below the hem. She froze.

Something happened.

The look in his eyes turned volcanic.

Somewhere in the back of her mind she was aware they stood just inside the doorway of a semi-crowded bar. Somewhere in her nonfunctioning gray matter she knew she'd only spoken a handful of sentences to this man. But somewhere in a part of her soul that had never been touched, a magnet flipped on and pulled her to this unselfish ranger.

When their lips connected, she forgot everything. She forgot the reason she was on lower Greenville. The reason she needed to leave. The reason she shouldn't be standing there kissing her escape plan.

Soft, firm lips grabbed hers, gently sucking and pulling. She parted her own. What should have been a strange invasion felt...perfect. His wonderfully strong arms reached around her body, pulling her into his hard angles. This wasn't kissing. It was more than fabulous. A simple lip-lock shouldn't make her weak in the knees.

"Get a room," someone in the bar shouted, followed by erupting laughter.

Wade's dark blue eyes watched her face as he pulled slightly away, his breathing just as rapid as hers. "Yours or mine?" he whispered, but the entire room listened.

Then she remembered the necessity to leave. Could the kiss have convinced Rushdan's men she'd really met her lover? Would sticking with him for a while save her life?

"Yours. Mine's too far," she heard herself say.

He didn't let her pull away. He kept her safely tucked into his side as they let the door close and headed toward a parking lot. That in itself was unusual... She wasn't used to someone else keeping *her* safe.

It had been a long time since she'd been nervous. What if they jumped them? Her Beretta was hidden in her car. The car several miles away. And now she'd involved an innocent man who had no idea what he'd just agreed to.

A slight laugh escaped. *Innocent?* The hunger in his eyes made her doubt her strong hero had ever been innocent.

Either way, she shouldn't involve him. It was against orders. She'd get to his truck and find another way out of this mess. But as they got outside, she looked up just as he glanced down. If she'd wanted to be heroic, she'd made a fatal mistake.

It happened again.

Raw energy pulled her to his mouth for a second time. He plunged between her lips, molded his hands to her butt and brought her into his instant hardness.

Someone cleared their throat. The sound jerked Wade away from her mouth, but not from her body. He kept her close, whispering what he wanted…what they'd eventually do. Small tremors shook from her into him. He skimmed her ear with his teeth.

There wasn't any doubt what would ultimately happen.

What they both needed.

Wade dug in his front pocket and shoved bills into the parking lot attendant's extended hand. Keeping his arm around her waist, he brought them both at a fast walk to his truck, forcing her to stay in step with him. Then he opened the driver's door and lifted her inside. She began slipping across the front seat, but spying Rushdan's men rounding the corner stopped her.

Before Wade could get the key in the ignition, she

pulled his face to hers, kissing him again but keeping her eyes on the men. Just like him.

Her rescuer pulled away, leaving both of them breathing hard. "I swear...if you keep kissing me like that, it won't matter what kind of favor you need me to do. We really will be heading straight for my place."

Chapter Three

Hell's bells, what was all that about? Wade couldn't wait for answers. The men following Therese were outside. Probably the reason Therese had kissed him again. And again.

She began to slide to the passenger side, but he stopped her, tugging her back to his hip. "Nope. You're staying right here. You aren't going anywhere without me. No disappearing acts."

"I was only getting a seat belt. We can't afford to be stopped by the police."

He reached to the far side of her, remembering the silky feel of her thigh. He took pleasure in skimming her hip while he dug between the seats for the middle belt, then fastened it, pulling it tight across her lap.

He put the truck in gear and pulled past the men she obviously knew. "So what's the problem? Or should I refer to it as a favor?"

"Oh, I think you noticed." She waved to the men. "I hate it when they think I need protection."

"Hold on a minute," he interrupted while pulling from the parking lot. "You might as well come clean,

Therese. You chose to bring me into this. Now give it to me straight. No sidestepping the truth. Those guys were not a protection detail."

"I understood when you indicated that you didn't want to get involved. You can't have it both ways. I respect that. If you drop me at a corner, I'll call a rideshare to get back to my apartment." She tried to put space between them. It didn't work.

"You aren't going anywhere. And I *am* involved. They just took pictures of me and my truck." He pointed to the last man to head to their vehicle. "It won't be long before they know who I am, where I live and what I do."

"Oh, God. I forgot you'd be in your truck instead of a government vehicle. I can fix this before anything happens. I promise."

"No fixes. I need the truth for once, without any stalls." They were still near the bar as he watched the men get into a car double-parked on the street.

They crept along at a snail's pace. If you were driving to a bar on Greenville, you couldn't get upset about not getting anywhere fast. It was just part of coming to this part of town on a Friday night. Everyone expected to be stuck and frustrated in happy-hour traffic. But it guaranteed that the two cars would be sticking close to his tail. Something he didn't mind for the moment.

Not if it finally got him information about Therese.

"Turn on a side street, speed up and lose them," she said, stretching a little closer so she could see out of the rearview mirror.

But he'd made up his mind. He deserved answers. He made a couple of turns and headed into downtown.

"Where are you going? Wade? Are you… Are you trying to keep them in sight?"

"I thought you said you were hungry." It was a stall, pure and simple. Not fooling her a lick, judging by the roll of her eyes.

"Right. So now you're interested?"

He couldn't see her face. She sat next to him, one arm around her waist and leaning into the other—fingers against her forehead. He had no gauge—no history—to know if she was serious or not.

"About what? Being hungry? I happen to eat regularly."

She turned to look behind her. "They're not even bothering to hide that they're following." She tugged her cell phone from a small pocket he hadn't noticed before.

Feeling like a kid on his first real date, he dropped his arm around Therese's shoulders at the next stoplight. He looked back and counted how many cars behind him the two threats were.

"Where did you want to go?"

"A fancy hotel?" She rubbed his knee, causing his mind to detour.

He kept driving. Proud that he didn't run off the road with all the distracting images he had running though his head. A protection detail or hit men? Could he keep her safe if they went to a… He swallowed hard and replayed her words.

Dammit—too much sarcasm.

"Okay. Enough games and put away that phone." He pulled through the light, slowing enough to make certain he was still followed until he had answers. "Maybe you should just tell me what's going on? And I mean everything, Therese. Don't leave out anything. You should consider me part of whatever operation you're running."

"I can tell you part of the story." She turned slightly, scraping her fingernails across his after-hours scruff.

"First." He squeezed her shoulder, tugging her slightly back to him. "You should probably know that if you invite me to a hotel again, I'm heading straight there. And don't plan on me sleeping anywhere except next to you."

She smiled. It might have even been genuine instead of completely calculated to capture his attention.

"And second?" she asked, outlining his ear with the tip of her finger.

He pulled to a stop at a red light. Her *friends* had moved closer—as in the car was now beside the truck. She looked at him and he prepared. The sultry lips were in front of his face, and her lips connected to his in slow motion. She kissed him deeply, deliberately and for longer than it took the light to turn green.

Horns honked. Both cars blocked a full one-way downtown street in Friday night traffic. Horns honked more. It registered in his mind, but he didn't want to let her go.

She slipped from his arms with a very satisfied grin. "They blinked."

"What?" He pulled forward on autopilot after the cars behind him veered around his truck.

"Drive slow and they'll have to pull through the next light. Then we're in the clear."

Oh, yeah, the men following her—them. Dammit, he'd completely lost focus. He couldn't blame anything except holding her—the only woman he'd thought about more than twice since meeting her.

"I think all the kissing fooled them," she said. "Oh great. They're pulling over to wait on us."

"We should use their following to our advantage," he threw out. How? He wasn't sure.

"What do you mean?"

"Tell me what's going on, beginning with the thugs behind us." He kept heading west on Commerce, past downtown, past the county jail. They stayed close on his tail, not trying to hide. "Are you in danger?"

"Short version?"

"We'll start with a simple yes or no."

"How about an *I think so*?"

"You've got to be kidding me. I need some answers, Therese. Or I'm making a U-turn back to County and a hundred police officers. You can try explaining to one of them. What will your friends do then?"

"No. Good grief, you don't have any right to make demands." She unfastened her seat belt, turned and brought a bare leg up next to his, dropping a hand in her lap and using the other to twirl her hair. "You know this is all your fault."

"My fault?" He couldn't let all that bare skin get under his. But it was definitely getting harder to concentrate. He should make her turn back around and refasten the belt.

"Asking around town for me actually got these guys all in my face. I wasn't prepared with answers and had to come up with some type of excuse."

"What the hell are you sidestepping, Therese?" Maybe his words could have been a little less confrontational, a little less loud. *Not really.* "Dammit, I need some answers."

"The truth is I've been on this case for over three years."

Case? Three years on a *case*? "I knew it." He slowed to a stop, wanting to caress all that silkiness. "You're undercover FBI. That's why you were with Steve Woods that day."

Her hands waved him to silence even as her lips puckered sexily again. "Shh. Don't say it aloud even if we're alone. When you started asking around town for me, I shrugged it off. But then you kept asking and it's made my 'boss'—" she shrugged, using air quotes to stress the word "—a little angsty."

"Angsty enough to send your um…protection detail?" Hit men, more like it. God, he wanted to pull her to him and kiss her. He shook it off. Men. Guns. Undercover. Favor. Focus.

"Last chance, Therese. Who is your boss?"

"What I'm working on isn't important."

"It is to me. I can keep my mouth shut. Secrets are easy."

"You can't mess this up, Wade. It took me over a year to work my way into Rushdan Reval's confidence. I just need you to stop asking—"

"You're working with Reval's group? So that's what you were doing when we arrested him last year? Have you been in Dallas this whole time without contacting me?"

"No…not…really." She stared him down like he was insane if he thought she'd hide from him.

"Don't try that look on me again, Therese. You have a successful disappearing act."

"I wanted to reach out, but I was given a direct order to avoid contact. It might have ruined my cover. After he was arrested, Rushdan pushed me off on one of his side gigs in San Antonio. I've been waiting for him to clear the charges you brought before I could continue here." She waved him forward with a finger. "You should probably keep driving even if we don't know where."

He'd sat through the light twice. Reval's men were hanging farther back, and as he moved forward through the yellow glow, they raced to catch him but got stuck instead.

"I know where I'm going. We need backup."

"No. Believe me. If they were going to attack, they would have by now," she said, looking back over his hand, still around her shoulder.

He retrieved his phone from his back pocket, reluctantly losing contact with Therese. "I need to take care of some cover issues before we go forward." He dialed Company B headquarters.

"Wade, seriously. I've been at this a long time. You've helped enough. I can't put you in danger again. Reval's going to recognize you as the Texas Ranger from last year." She sat straight on the seat, scooting toward the passenger door.

No!

"Dammit, Therese, there's no reason for you to jump out in the middle of nowhere. I can hide us for a few days until we sort out what to do."

He reached out to grab her arm and missed before she opened the door. Therese could probably jump—he'd slowed for a curve—but he slammed on the brakes so she wouldn't have to.

"Just keep driving, Wade. They won't bother you if I'm not here."

Out in a flash, she passed the truck and ran for a path between the trees. He couldn't follow her before he parked. And as soon as he did, they'd know they were out of the truck. Speeding up, he was far enough ahead of the men following that he could whip into a warehouse lot and cut his engine before he was seen.

"Dammit. Razor wire." He couldn't go over and had to go out through the same gate he'd come in. They'd probably see him if he did. *You are not disappearing on me again, Therese Ortis.* "Not this time."

He couldn't make his customized truck disappear or blend in with the others taking up the spaces. The built-in compartments made it impossible to mistake. And Therese was right, several of Reval's men would recognize it as belonging to the ranger they'd captured last year after he'd taken out one of their men.

There was an upside to him being in his truck—the built-in gun safe holding his weapon. But if he pursued Therese on foot without notifying headquarters… If things went haywire… If he messed up an FBI undercover operation…

No more being a Texas Ranger. He was done.

Was she worth it? He didn't need a thoughtful reflection. There wasn't a choice. He needed her safe.

"If I didn't owe her my life, I could drive away and do nothing." He eased from the truck. "Hell."

The longer he took to make a decision, the farther Therese got ahead of him.

So be it. There were a lot of *ifs* in his life. *If* he hadn't made a couple of scenes looking for her during the past six weeks…she would have blown him off forever. And *if* Therese hadn't come to his rescue by contacting Jack last year… Well, he wouldn't be here now, needing to make a decision.

Keeping his head down, he retrieved his weapon. He couldn't go over the eight-foot fence, or around it. Not with the thug car just outside the gate—not without the thugs seeing and following. Okay. Then he'd just have to go through the building and find a rear exit. He could make it to the open loading dock door.

That was all. Cross an open parking lot directly in front of the two cars and jump onto the four-foot loading dock without being seen. He didn't trust Therese's opinion about being safe. He couldn't get

caught. Once these yahoos realized who he was…
he'd be dead. Therese, too. When they caught her.

One step at a time. A honk from a big rig made
the car that had followed them pull to the side of the
road closest to the lot.

But the eighteen-wheeler pulled inside the gate,
effectively allowing him to cross the lot without the
thugs seeing him. He kept running until he passed
two building doors. The third had the street view
blocked by a box truck. Once he made it there, it was
easy to enter the loading bay. He casually walked
through the manufacturing company's warehouse.
Few people were around as he made his way to the
west side of the building, which backed up to the
railroad.

He needed wire cutters or something to get
through the fence. Nothing. Noticing a man taking
his cigarettes from his pocket and heading to an outside door, Wade followed and took a look.

There was a gate. So instead of sulking around
kicking himself, he made his job work for him. He
headed straight to the office.

"Man, am I glad you're open twenty-four hours,"
he entered. "Texas Rangers, ma'am." He flipped open
his creds. "Would you happen to have a key to your
back gate?"

Chapter Four

The evening hour had made it easy for Therese to hide. Unfortunately, it made it terribly difficult to move through the brush. The heels didn't help, either. She pulled them off, looping a finger in each strap to carry them. They were too expensive to leave behind and a pair of her favorites. Slowly picking her way from one oak to the next, she carefully walked through the dirt and debris, hoping for a path.

Far from a Dallas city park, the two ruts were about the same distance apart as a four-wheeler. Nothing was around. Even the ambient light from the city was getting scarce. As scarce as her dress that snagged on every tree she passed.

Another rip and she groaned. "Shoot. What a night to wear the sexiest thing I own."

"It is really sexy."

Her heart leaped into her throat. She totally understood what that meant now as her pulse beat at an insane pace. "Oh my God, Wade. You scared me. What are you doing here?"

"Right. I scared you." Wade grabbed her hand.

"What the hell, Therese? You jumped out of my truck."

"If you get involved with this—"

"I already am."

"I admit that it was stupid to march into that bar and ask you for anything. Whatever you're thinking, you don't owe me. You have no obligation. Nothing. Do you hear me?"

"Everybody will hear you if you don't keep your voice down. Your friends found my truck and caught on that we're out here in the trees."

"And if you'd kept driving like I meant for you to…they would have followed you until it was too late to realize I was no longer there."

"Pardon me, but you didn't ask me to keep driving. What you did was apologize."

"I don't apologize."

"Well, you did to me." His voice was louder.

"Shh." She couldn't kiss him into silence this time.

It didn't matter. He took her hand, leading her away from the sounds of men tromping through the brush somewhere behind her. They ran and the sounds of the men searching for them grew fainter, but Wade kept pushing forward.

"How did you find me?" she whispered. "Ow. Hey, slow down."

"What's wrong?"

She pushed her high heels into his chest. He pushed them right back, then bent in half. Oh, Lord. He stifled her gasp when his hands touched her backside as he lifted her, with the pressure of his shoulder cutting off a lot of her air.

Hearing above the truck traffic on the nearby road grew more difficult, but voices seemed to carry. She had an unusual view behind them to see if they were being followed. No one seemed to be around.

"Um... Wade, honey?" she chastised as his fingers slid under her dress to stabilize her on his shoulder.

"Oh, pardon me." He laughed.

The thong only covered so much. Embarrassingly, he'd found a whole lot of nothing. He continued to carry her toward the open railroad tracks. No cover put them at a greater risk.

She tapped on his back. "Come on, put me down. No one's following."

"Are you sure you can walk?"

He did a deep knee bend, pulling her dress down, then smoothing it over both hips as her feet hit the ground. After all the kisses she'd laid on him, she deserved whatever teasing he dished out. The playfulness between them had been there since the very first phone call.

This was all her fault. She couldn't stop encouraging him. She slipped her shoes back on her feet, admitting two things. No matter how expensive the shoes were, they could never be worn in public again. And she didn't want to stop whatever attraction she had for this man.

"I really shouldn't have involved you in this."

"Better than paperwork." He shrugged. "No need

to beat a dead horse, Therese. I'm here. I'm involved. Let's deal with it and get out of here."

They'd both been talking in a loud whisper, but noises from the trees had them shutting their mouths and running—even in heels along the train tracks. Hitting the old wood slats was much faster than trudging through the washed-out gravel, and they could avoid the risk of stepping in a hole and turning an ankle.

"We're almost at Westmoreland Road," she told him over her shoulder.

"Your friends are catching up. Will they shoot?" Wade's question was answered with a couple of rounds from a handgun.

"Head for the far trees," Wade yelled.

To hell with the shoes. She kicked them off, leaving them as they ran full out for the trees to their right. She couldn't be bothered with how much the gravel hurt her feet. If she stopped, Rushdan's men would capture her. She might survive to be taken back to the slimy pig, but Wade probably wouldn't. He'd die before he let those men take her.

That was the kind of guy he was. Honorable. Trustworthy.

"Stop whatever you're thinking and head down the tracks. We'll never make those trees," he said. "I've got this."

"How?"

"I came prepared. Just run to the right once you hit the street." He pulled his phone from his back pocket.

More shots.

The industrial area allowed them only one direction left to run. They were boxed in by the grove of trees behind and on either side businesses with eight-foot fences and razor wire on top.

Rushdan's men were too close behind them. The only direction left was the open area along the railroad tracks until they crossed Westmoreland Street. Then where?

She hit the sidewalk and turned right as Wade instructed. He stopped at the fence pole—as if that would stop a bullet—and fiddled with his phone.

"Keep moving to the intersection!" he told her.

The men following shot again. "Come on." She tugged on his elbow.

"Get going. I'm right behind you." He waved his hand holding the cell and leaned around the poll.

She was out of breath and her feet were hurting enough to make her scream, but she ran the long block to the intersection. Still half a block behind her, Wade waved her forward.

"Go on! Cross!"

The light was in her favor, so she ran…again. And kept running to the brick wall of the small convenience store. Wade received honks from the cars he darted in front of. Rushdan's men didn't follow him.

"Where to now?" She gulped air into her lungs. "Were you calling for backup or 911? Do you think anyone else did?"

"Our ride's here." He waved his phone at a sedan pulling into a parking space.

"This is a bad idea. We can't involve a ride-for-hire driver."

"It's only a short distance. Or would you rather run? Your *friends* are probably getting into their cars now."

"This is really dangerous."

He blocked her from view and tilted her face to look at him. "Do we blow your cover?" he asked in a whisper.

"Over three years of undercover work..." She hesitated.

"I don't think anyone has seen us, but we've got to go. Now." He drew her to him and gave her lips a quick kiss as if they'd known each other for years.

"Take the car and get as far away from me as possible. Leave town. Go on vacation. Let me talk my way out of this with Rushdan."

"Isn't he the one who sent these guys to take you out? You gotta let me help with this, Therese." He laced his fingers through hers and opened the car door, helping her inside.

"Evenin'," the driver said. "You going to the Westin at the Galleria mall?"

"That's right," Wade answered.

"Wait a minute. Isn't that a hotel?" She remembered his promise. And by the twinkle in his eye, so did he.

"Funny you should mention that." Wade winked.

"They're going to find out where we've gone," she told him.

"I'm counting on it. But to give us a little time..."

He tapped the front seat to get the driver's attention, then showed him his credentials. "This is going to sound weird. I need you to take the long way through downtown."

"Whatever you want, but it'll cost more."

"If someone asks where you dropped us, just tell them. There's no reason to be a hero. Okay?"

"You got it. But how long of a ride are you talking?"

Wade tugged her securely into his arms and tilted her lips to his. "As long as it takes."

"Sure, man. Anything for law enforcement."

"This is insane," she whispered against his lips. "Are you seriously going to neck with me in the back seat of a rideshare car while Rushdan's men try to find us?"

"As soon as I use the credit card in my wallet, they'll know where we are. Besides…when's the last time you had some fun in the back seat?" He pulled her onto his lap and devoured her mouth until she gently pushed against his chest.

"You know we'll most likely be dead tomorrow. Since this is the last bit of pleasure either of us will ever enjoy…I'm in."

Chapter Five

"This won't work," Jack MacKinnon yelled through the phone.

"Sure it will. You're mainly angry because you'll have to work all night to make it happen. Give me some bad debt, add a couple of reprimands to my file— Okay, a couple more reprimands. It'll give me a reason to need money. I've got the setup from last year when that stuff with Megan went down."

"I think they hit you one too many times on your head. That *stuff* is when they tried to kill you. Remember how these same people were going to drop a building on top of you as your tomb?"

He rubbed his ribs. "It's hard to forget."

"This is a bad idea."

"I keep telling him that," Therese said from beside him.

"You're on speaker. She insisted on listening in," he told his partner. "I've got a hunch that you're giving in, Jack. You know it's a good idea. It's logical and if you get the finances falsified, Rushdan Reval will be completely suckered in."

"Your hunches have been close to getting us both killed, pal."

"You'll do it?"

"You two can't be serious. You're both crazy." Therese walked away from the phone, throwing up her hands and heading to the bath. "You *are* crazy, Wade. Major Clements will never go for this," Jack said.

"He will if you plead the case. What can I do? She's the woman who saved your girlfriend and me. Remember? Don't you think you owe her?"

A long, indecisive sigh from his partner filled the dead air. "You know that favor you owe me, Wade?"

"What favor?" Yeah, he knew full well what Jack meant.

"Remember when you asked me to pick a woman up from the airport. No big deal, you said. Keep her out of trouble, you said. Out of sight until I hear from you again. No big deal."

Wade took him off speaker. He knew exactly what Jack was recounting. Therese did, too, since she was the person who'd asked him to protect her friend.

Out of the blue, Therese had asked for a strange favor. After all was said and done, the Company B Rangers had discovered that Megan Harper's life had been in danger. Jack had saved her. Sure that Therese had been in trouble, Wade had searched for her, gotten caught and been beaten within an inch of his life.

"Look how good that turned out for you, Jack. You met your future wife."

Wade's occasional banter and favors for Therese

had become an obsession to find her. But she'd really disappeared.

"Ha. I think it's time for me to redeem a favor from you."

"Yeah, I remember owing you a favor. But I thought you'd ask me to pay for the limo at your wedding or something." He had to dig deep in order to convince Jack to help. Time to make the big man feel indebted. "Okay, I sort of promised I'd never mention this again. But Therese is the one who saved you from MS-13 when your dad blew your cover."

"How? I thought you said... Dammit, Wade. You never mentioned where that helicopter came from. Therese was the one who arranged it?"

"I didn't ask who it belonged to. She didn't say. I just found out she has access to privileged information. That's when I knew. Now you do, too."

"She saved my hide and then Megan's." Jack sighed again. "And yours."

Wade looked around at the closed bathroom door. "She won't admit it, but I think she's in trouble. Big trouble. She's afraid to go to the FBI or any other backup she has."

"Is she afraid of a breach?"

"Jack, why else would she have come to me?"

"Right. She trusts you. I get it. I'll get Heath onto your finances. He's going to love working all night. What kind of problem do you want? Gambling would be the easiest."

Gambling. It hit a nerve he'd kept buried for a decade. He didn't want to slip back into the familiar world. But he could to save their lives.

On their way to the hotel they'd shared a lot of kisses and a few whispers of how to convince Reval not to kill them. It was up to him—and a fake financial background—to prove he was dirty. A dirty Texas Ranger who needed quick cash and was willing to do anything for anybody. Including the man who'd ordered his death last year.

It turned his stomach, but it would work.

"Sure. Just as long as Heath can—and will—make it all go away. I'm going silent. I'm locking my stuff in the safe. Send someone to pick it up."

"Watch your back."

Wade turned his phone off. It was the best he could do.

"About that explanation..." He poked his head between the bathroom door and the frame.

Therese was under the streaming water, naked like she should be for a shower, her long hair flowing down her back. Her arms were raised to her face just enough for him to see the curve of her breast and lots of smooth skin.

"Sorry." He averted his eyes to the bottom of the towel hanging on the wall rack. "I heard the water running and expected the shower curtain. Not clear doors."

"No need to be embarrassed. I think our relationship is far beyond professional. Don't you?" She turned the interesting parts of her body toward the back wall.

He could see the outline of her legs and her beautifully shaped derriere. Had he just thought all the interesting parts were facing the other way?

"You know that I didn't mean that stuff about the hotel. Right? I'm fine sleeping in the chair." He stepped backward to give her privacy and to stop acting like an ogling lecher.

"Maybe we should talk about this in a minute? You're letting in a cold draft." She laughed at him.

"Got it. I'll order us some food."

"Or you could join me," she teased.

Against every desire he had, he managed to close the door. The first time he made love to Therese, it wouldn't be while they waited on Reval's men to take them to the second-rate crime boss. He ordered two steaks and the works, hoping that the woman he'd been kissing for the past hour wasn't a vegetarian. He didn't know a thing about her.

"Oh, man, I feel better." She was wrapped in a towel, her wet hair slicked back, and her bare arms raised to pat the long strands dry with a second towel. "I am so starved. I had to skip lunch today."

She looked at the dress, now with several tears on the sides. The towel slipped. He lost his concentration as she caught it, tugging the end back into place.

"What food did you order?" she asked, laughing as she sat on the edge of the bed next to him.

He jumped up. "We should probably keep some distance between us." He pulled his dress shirt from his shoulders and handed it to her.

How did she stay cool about being naked under

that towel? A little towel that would drop from her body with a gentle tug.

"Such unusual modesty as he takes his shirt off. This coming from the guy who just necked with me for the half-hour drive." She bent her arm and hooked her long hair that was beginning to curl behind her ear.

Did she have curly hair?

"This is different," he finally got out.

"You could have fooled me. Our rideshare driver had a lot of fun watching."

God, he loved her laugh. She didn't do that enough. He turned his back, shutting his eyes tight while she put his shirt on.

"Maybe you should tell me about Reval and how he fits in with Public Exposure? Yeah, I connected those dots. Last time I saw you we just took down part of that domestic terrorism group. Is Reval working for them or vice versa?"

"You're right. We've had credible intel for quite a while—"

"The beginning, remember?" he interrupted. He wanted every piece of information she had. "Who's 'we'? And how long have you been under, working with that scumbag?"

"I'll save the real beginning for another time. Sharing this amount of the intel will probably get me fired."

"Hey, it won't matter if we're dead like you keep telling me." He wished room service would knock on the door. He wanted a beer in his hand.

"That's true. But since you've put yourself in the middle of everything, you probably should know what's going on." She covered her face with her hands, then crossed her fingers on both sides of her face with a very fake smile. "I sure hope you're a good liar, Wade Hamilton."

"I can fake it when necessary."

"Great. If you can't, we really don't stand a chance." She stood. "Turn around."

He obliged but saw an arm extend through a blue sleeve.

"All done." She wandered around the room examining fliers and hotel info, straightened the lamp and discovered robes in the closet. A robe she didn't put on until room service arrived.

When the robe was safely around her body, relief washed over him along with the smell of food. His stomach growled as he signed for the feast. They settled on either side of the bed with two trays set between them.

"Back to our story," he urged. "From the beginning."

"I was at the police academy in San Antonio. I guess I fit the profile of someone the FBI needed. Honestly, I don't know why they chose me over anyone else," Therese said between bites.

"Is that where you met Jack's girlfriend, Megan?"

"Yes. Everyone was told that I was forced to drop out after cheating or something. The Bureau used that when Rushdan—or anyone else—checked out my background."

He knew that partly from Megan, partly because it was so prominent in any report on her that he'd initiated. "So you went to work for the FBI?"

"They wanted to discover where Rushdan's money came from and who his contacts were."

"Let me guess, a little drug running, real estate fraud, night clubs, prostitution and money laundering."

"You did your homework." She clapped softly.

"I have a tendency to obsess over people who try to kill me." Was it too soon to say he'd actually been looking for her?

"Did your research mention that Rushdan Reval has been brokering illegal deals? I never discovered how he got into it. But last year, when his real estate fraud fell apart, he began contact with Public Exposure."

"That's how a low-level fraud group got into the domestic terrorism business?"

"When Megan and Jack stumbled on Rushdan's real estate fraud, it stalled my involvement. At least with his Dallas group. I mainly played go-between on the phone with several of his *business* representatives in San Antonio."

"That's stating it nicely."

"True." She stuffed a yeast roll in her mouth, swishing it down with a cola—not the beer.

"Let me guess… Enter FBI agent Kendall Barlow and her husband Texas Ranger Heath Murray, investigating claims about Public Exposure's fraud."

She pointed at him. "Yes! Bonus points for the

man without a shirt. They really are a good team.
Almost too good, since they practically dismantled
the Brantley Lourdes end of this thing."

"Brantley Lourdes. Isn't he the guy in charge of
Public Exposure? And what do you mean *almost*?
We retrieved the algorithm, obtained confessions
and nothing happened after all the threats that Dallas citizens would die."

"That's the problem. Rushdan just brokered the
deal for Public Exposure. He only had a copy. Someone else developed the algorithm. Sources have
verified that he's improved it and bidding for the
improved version has begun. We're no longer certain what the algorithm is capable of."

"Son of a biscuit eater!" He picked up his roll.
"Lourdes wouldn't tell you who created it? I thought
this case was wrapped up. I haven't seen any alerts
from local, state or national authorities. Why are your
bosses being so secretive?"

"Do you really not know after one of the FBI's
Dallas agents was caught in the middle of this?"

"I get it. There might be another traitor around.
But you trust me, right? I could have been helping
discover who Reval plans to sell to."

"I've already explained why working with you
wasn't possible. Besides that information isn't what
we're after. We need to discover what it does now.
In addition to capturing the geeks who designed an
algorithm that can take down a city's electrical grid."

"Every city's worst nightmare."

"Country's worst nightmare. I've been attempting to get back in Rushdan's good graces. He's accused me of helping you escape, but he seems to overlook it."

"Why's that?"

"Maybe he's hoping I'll hang myself and he won't have to give the order to get rid of me. Like other people I won't name…" Therese reached over the tray and brushed crumbs from the corner of his mouth, seductively raising an eyebrow in his direction "…he's sort of sweet on me."

Man alive, he no longer wanted to talk about Rushdan Reval or the FBI or algorithms that could bring down cities or countries. At her touch, he just wanted to pull her to the bed and finish a different discussion.

"You know, it's not too late for you to go back to your regular duties as a Texas Ranger. I can clean this up."

"No. We talked about this." He stood, removing the remnants of dinner to the desk. "I'm going with you and we'll find the threat. I've spoken with Jack. I'll call back. Who should he speak with at the FBI to confirm my involvement?"

"Steve Woods. He's the only person I can trust there who knows about the threat. He's working with Homeland and only providing 'as needed' info to them."

"You don't trust very easily, do you?"

"No," she answered with a whisper. "Rushdan will have a hard time believing a big ol' Texas Ranger is willing to get his hands dirty. Why is that exactly?"

"Money. It's always about money."

"We'll have to convince him you need a lot… and fast."

"Right. Heath will be set before Reval looks into my background." He pushed down the old feelings from his youth. Fright had no place here. He needed confidence and arrogance. "Think I have time for a shower before our location is discovered?"

"Probably. I think I'll try to catch some sleep. After they get here, it might be rough." She draped the robe across the end of the bed, then pulled back the covers. "Thank you."

"For what?" he asked from the bathroom door.

The urge to bring her close was overwhelming. His knuckles turned white as he gripped the door trim and tried to keep himself there instead of at her side. She smiled—completely sexy in his blue shirt that looked better on her than him. That was all she did, but he understood.

He took a quick shower, thinking about the impossible situation the FBI and Homeland had placed on her shoulders. Therese needed help whether anyone admitted it or not.

Her eyes were closed when he locked his phone, gun and creds inside the safe. He called Jack from the hotel line—not only to check in, but to tell him the combination so he could send one of the guys to grab his things.

He scrambled back into his jeans since he knew that at some point a gun would be aimed and they'd be taken to Reval's headquarters. Therese shivered in her sleep. He smoothed the covers and she backed her body close to his. They lay in each other's arms, fitfully resting. He woke with every movement and could tell that she hadn't fallen into a deep sleep, either. He kept her close, whispering again what he would eventually do.

Around four in the morning, Reval's men arrived for the next phase of their undertaking. It was going to be a very long day.

Chapter Six

Rushdan's men used a key to enter the hotel room. Wade covered Therese with the robe as the door burst open, so he hadn't been taken by surprise.

He'd held on to her body until they were yanked apart and his hands tied behind his back, angled to grab her robe before she was shoved through the door.

Therese had never worked with a partner and oddly enjoyed the thought of her first being this tall Texas Ranger. She liked him. A lot.

All those sexy words he'd whispered in her ear as she'd tried to go to sleep still had her body burning. She hadn't dare tell him she wanted the same. She wouldn't have held back. If they survived, being with Wade would be a genuine pleasure.

But one that would wait.

It was infuriating not to be tied up like Wade, not to be considered a threat. But she'd worked hard over the last years not to reveal her strength or quickness to these men. She walked freely as they were taken down the service elevator and escorted into the back of an SUV.

Once they were at Rushdan's new office, one of his hired goons punched Wade hard enough to make him lose his breath. "That was for the six months I served in the county jail."

What had she done by involving Wade? How could she have let her judgment lapse so badly not once but several times? She'd completely lost her mind and would probably lose her job for disclosing everything about her undercover assignment.

But worse…if they beat Wade or tortured him? Would she be able to hold her tongue?

"Just take us to Rushdan," she instructed, stepping in front of Wade. "If you touch my boyfriend again, I guarantee you won't be around tomorrow to regret it."

Therese held her breath, preparing for the punch that never came—not to her and not a second one to Wade, either. Both of them knew the risks. Talking his way into the Reval organization was a long shot. They were both flanked by two men who yanked them through rooms and eventually stood them in front of Rushdan Reval.

"Therese, my darling. Come, let me see you. Untie our guest." Reval instructed his men. "Are you barbarians or something just as awful?"

The goons released her arms when she gave them a shrug. She approached Reval's desk wearing the robe over Wade's shirt, which covered her skimpy underwear.

"Come closer. You know what I want." The pig tugged at the belt at her waist, inching her closer to his chair. She could see his hope of anticipation that she'd let the robe fall open. She dug her fingers into the cotton sides, barely keeping it closed.

Somehow she managed to get into character, the part she played of a dingy woman who was slightly incompetent. The character that all these men thought so little about that they didn't bother to tie her hands.

Tonight was different. Wade watched, as well. His strength could be felt across the room. She saw the worry on the men's faces. Gritting her teeth, she forced herself to tolerate Rushdan as he unbuttoned the top two buttons of the dark blue dress shirt. He skimmed the back of his fingers against her cleavage to cop a filthy feel. She desperately wanted to slap his hands away from her, but she took it.

Just like always.

The men gripping Wade attempted to hold him, but he broke free. He yanked her back to his arms just before the robe fell open.

"So it's true. Our ranger friend has a thing for you. After all this time of you saying no to me, you said yes to someone who can put you behind bars? Do you think he really cares for you?"

"He got me out of jail last year."

"So you finally admit that you had someone with pull to help you. Why not just tell me the multiple times I've asked?"

"He said it was a secret, Rushy, baby. And you told me secrets were important," she sounded more like the confused ditz they were used to. "I told you I was meeting someone last night and you had me followed. I don't understand what I did wrong."

"They ran." The bigger-than-big man tsked at them.

"Only after they began shooting at us," Wade threw out.

"I didn't ask you, ranger boy." Rushdan dug his fingernail into his mouth, picking food from his teeth, then gestured as if shooing a fly. "Take him from my sight while I decide what to do with him. Did you think to bring their clothes?"

"Rushdan, baby." Therese turned and took steps back to her "boss," letting the robe fall open, and purposely tugging the shirt to where it left little to the pig's imagination. "I've been working on this guy for months. I thought you could use his help."

All the men in the room could barely raise their eyes. She had them mesmerized and hoping the shirt would fall completely open. Rushdan had the best seat.

The pig.

"I spent nearly six months in that filthy cell, wearing orange." He shuddered. "Why would you think you could bring your pet in here for me to adopt? I have no use for a Texas Ranger. He can't do anything for me. Even if I thought he really would." Rushdan tried for a whimsical, light voice, but it was countered by the evil in his eyes.

"You're right. I didn't believe Wade at first, either. Now I mainly want the money he owes me."

She leaned forward to whisper. Rushdan bent to look down her shirt. "He has a gambling problem, baby. You can use that against him," she suggested.

"Therese." Once again Wade tugged on her arm to pull her to his side. "I can speak for myself."

"Not if he won't listen, sugar."

"Aww, how sweet. The two lovebirds are fighting," Rushdan said.

"We aren't fighting." Wade buttoned the shirt to cover her cleavage. She spun around while he kept his hands on her shoulders.

"I do so enjoy your little shows, Therese. Too bad it seems your champion has ended this one." He nodded to his men. "I'm busy. Go put them somewhere until I'm not."

"But," she began again.

"By the way, I love the boots. Sal, remind me I need to get me some real Texas boots." He pointed at Wade's Western footwear.

"Yes, sir." Sal pushed at them with a gun.

Rushdan looked at the men in the room. "I said put them somewhere until I can think up an appropriate punishment."

Therese forced Wade to let go of her. "Really, Rushdan. I do a good job for you. Even while you were gone I ran the San Antonio clubs like you wanted. Wade is a fun time, but you know I'm loyal to you. I really thought we could use his connections to widen our prospects."

"Why would you think that?" Rushdan said,

smacking his lips after another bite of breakfast. "Or should I ask why you try to think at all?"

"I thought I could help."

"Therese, you are such a nice-looking broad. But why do you bother?" Rushdan backhanded her, sending her stumbling barefoot against Wade.

She quickly turned around and stopped the ranger from roaring forward. "I warned you about this, Wade," she whispered. "Rushdan is always right and never wrong."

"I can't let him—"

She locked both his hands with hers. But he still managed to swoosh her around and protect her, absorbing Rushdan's next blow across his back.

"I need the money," Wade managed after a couple of seconds. "I admit that. Thing is, Texas Rangers are squeaky clean, man. No one thinks of us as being dishonest. It doesn't happen. You're throwing something special away here, Reval. I'm a one-of-a kind opportunity. Whatever you think up, I can do."

"Wait, wait, wait," Therese said as Sal began pushing them from the room. "Please listen. He can get inside places even the cops you own can't get into. Wade literally works with every agency. Right?"

"All right. Wait. Can you really get inside every building or restricted area?"

Yes! They'd found a reason Wade was unique.

"Sure. No problem." Wade shrugged.

"How do I know this isn't just a very good acting job?" Rushdan swiveled his huge body to sit in his chair. His house slippers slid across the marble floor.

Only the best for Rushdan Reval.

Wade slipped his arm around her waist. "I can't help it. No way can I walk away from this lady. I'm crazy about her. Thing is, she doesn't come cheap. I need money, Reval. If I don't work for you, I'll be working for someone else to get it."

Oh, God, he was about to kiss her. She recognized that smoldering longing in his eyes. How in the world could he do that with threats and guns hanging over them?

"This just might work, but what type of collateral can you give me?" Her enemy interrupted.

"Collateral, sir?"

"Aren't you quaint. *Sir?*" Rushdan looked around at his men. "Listen to that, he called me *sir* and actually means it. Yes, collateral. You don't think I'm going to invest in you so you can steal from me when you're entrusted with something valuable, do you? I don't work that way."

"Me," she answered for Wade. "I'll be his collateral."

"Isn't that sweet." Rushdan used his pinky to pick something from his teeth again, making the nice words turn sour. "Unfortunately Therese, you're already mine. Neither important nor valuable."

"She is to me. I love her."

The words struck something deep inside her. Even knowing they were said in order to save their lives. Coming from his lips after the beautiful night in the hotel…she realized just how much she wanted them to be true.

Chapter Seven

"Take them somewhere." Rushdan shooed his crew away like they were flies. The thud of someone being shoved reminded him to say, "And no punching. At least not yet. Pretty boy might have a job to do."

He caught Sal's look, which certainly questioned his temporary decision. He hated anyone questioning him. What was the harm of considering the ranger's proposition? If he didn't, he'd lose Therese, too.

One person could give him the confirmation he needed. Andrew was faster with a computer than Rushdan was at making money. He silently laughed at his own joke and picked up his normal phone. Then dialed the number on the hidden cell phone in his desk.

The key to everything was right there in plain sight for anyone who wanted to see it. But they wouldn't know what it was and they wouldn't know what to say even if they found a reason to search.

"Money is a pitiless master but a zealous servant." The code quote seemed both stupid and cryptic.

"P.T. Barnum," the voice answered. "Andrew, it's

for you," the voice called from a distance a few seconds later.

He looked around the new office, so close in style to his last. A shame he'd blown up the previous one. All because that badass ranger had brought others to try and take him down. Perhaps this was a mistake and he should just kill him and be done with it.

Therese would need to die, too.

He tapped on the fish tank full of smaller versions of the inhabitants of the one he'd had last year. They'd gain in size, just like his bank roll would after this deal was brokered. The biggest deal of his life.

"Yeah?" Andrew finally said.

"This is Rushdan Reval. I need information on Wade Hamilton. He's a Texas Ranger in Dallas." Rushdan waited for some type of acknowledgment.

"Who is this? JK, I mean…just kidding, Reval. What did you want?" Andrew asked.

"I need information. Today."

"Yeah, on a Texas Ranger. You said that. Why are you bothering, Reval? Does it have anything to do with our deal?"

"As a matter of fact, I either need to kill him or I can use him to help facilitate the exchange."

"I'll get back to you."

The phone went dead. "Thank you, I look forward to hearing from you," he said into the phone, refusing to let anyone working for him know that someone had hung up on him.

Andrew was a rude young man who continued to

call him by his last name. No matter how many times he insisted on being called Rushdan.

"What now?" Sal asked. "I locked them in the sixth-floor storage room."

"Do you have surveillance in that room?"

"That's not up and running yet, boss."

"Dammit, Sal, make that a priority. I want to know if anyone is following our two guests or approaching our building."

"You got it, boss."

"Did anyone pick up his vehicle?"

"Nope."

Rushdan tapped on the glass. He didn't allow anyone else to bother his fish that way, but he loved it. They all swam toward him, expecting food.

"I guess a little more won't hurt you," he said to his fish. "Did you keep someone at the hotel room?"

"No. Want me to send someone back?"

"Why do I surround myself with idiots?"

The exception was Therese. Smart. Competent. Reliable. Even though she pretended to be all too stupid around his men. She had all the qualities that made him question why she worked for him. Even if she did try to hide behind the dumb broad persona she portrayed. He didn't understand why she played that part. It didn't make sense. And that was exactly the reason his men had been following her tonight.

He had suspicions. Too many coincidences for his peace of mind.

If he dwelled on it or questioned her motives too

much, he might let his paranoia get rid of her. But he wanted her in every way.

He should kill the ranger and be done with that specific problem. Sal and others had wanted him to deal with Therese after the Public Exposure episode but he'd ignored them.

The problem with Therese... She was good with the details. He needed her back in the fold and she might leave if anything happened to her "boyfriend."

"Oh, well," he mumbled to the blue fish with dots. "I shall call you Dotty."

If Wade Hamilton hadn't stuck his nose where it didn't belong last year, Rushdan would have his lovely office building, and the program would be complete for the new buyers. The money he would rake in from this deal would easily make up for the past six months of being shut down.

If he had a way to keep the ranger under his control, to assure that he'd behave, then he'd control Therese at the same time.

He tapped on the fish tank glass again. A beautiful blue-and-pink wrasse came to his finger. The blue reminded him of Therese's eyes. He'd have to ask her to streak that dark brown hair of hers pink. That would be interesting...very interesting.

Perhaps keeping the ranger alive could get him benefits of a different, more intimate nature with the smart beauty. Even if it didn't, having someone to offer his new clients assistance with their government endeavors would only help the real operation get up and running again. An inside man always paid off.

"Yes," he answered his beeping cell.

"Your ranger is in debt up to his eyeballs," Andrew said without any greeting. "That should be enough for your purposes. But I went a little deeper, just to make sure. Back to a sealed court case when he was fifteen. Seems he had a very big bad gambler dude for a daddy."

"Is he still alive?"

"Naw. Died in prison. But get why he was in the pen. The dude pulled the trigger on a Texas Ranger when a scam went south."

Blackmail. How convenient.

"Send me details. Everything."

"Look, Reval. My boss overheard the convo. Is the date firm yet?"

"Definitely. I'll have details first thing in the morning. It seems I have a new knight to insert into the game."

"Info is on its way. Did I mention my boss is getting impatient?"

And once again, Andrew disconnected without a proper goodbye, taking him by surprise. It didn't matter since he was alone. Sal had backed out of the room at his earlier irritation. A few arrangements and he'd get his gambling ranger involved so deep that the success of the deal would be guaranteed.

Chapter Eight

One dim yellow light in the back ceiling gave the small room an eerie feel. She sat next to Wade on the unfinished floor. At least it was cool against her bare legs. She pulled the belt on the robe tight again. Thank God Wade had given her his shirt or she might be even more exposed.

"Who has a storage closet that's completely empty?" she asked to break the silence.

"Reval seems to like 'em," Wade said quietly. "I was locked in one just like this."

"Oh, right. Sorry. That's where they kept you in the building that exploded."

"Don't forget I nearly exploded with it." He looped his fingers through hers, drawing her hand to his lips. "I should have said thanks as soon as I saw you again. You know…for getting me rescued."

"Are you really angry about me not calling you?"

"Did behaving like a hurt kid give me away?"

"Sort of." She patted his thigh like they'd been together for months, not hours. "So how do we get out of here?"

The electrical charge she associated with him filled the air as he leaned close enough to kiss her. His warm breath shifted to her neck and close to her ear. "We don't. Remember? We want to be right where we are."

"Don't we need a backup plan or something?"

"Shh." He placed a finger across her lips. "Your boss might be listening."

"I feel like we're wasting time," she whispered back, as close to his ear as he'd been to hers.

"I know a lot of things we can do in the dark."

His whisper sent one of those delicious tingles down her spine, landing in all the right spots.

"You already passed on that, remember?"

"Postponed," he breathed intimately across the top of her ear.

One word of encouragement from him and she melted in anticipation. About to give in, she came to her senses when two unknown somebodies walked past the door. "You're right. They may be watching us. I know surveillance and security increased since you brought the building down. Literally."

"To be fair, I was in no shape to destroy anything." Wade twisted her hair around his finger, trapping her ear close to his face.

"Never mind, you know exactly what I mean." Breathy words escaped and a gasp of expectation as his lips passed across hers once more.

"As a matter of fact, I do," he said louder, leaning away from her.

"Don't sound so surprised." She cut an anxious

giggle short, changing it to a worried tap on his shoulder. *Why am I more nervous with him than the criminal I work for?*

"I am surprised."

"Why? This happens when two people know each other. It's natural."

He laughed so hard he began to choke, coughing into his hand like a man with asthma.

"Why is that so funny?" she asked before she laughed with him.

"Therese, we don't know each other." He shook his head, laughing more. "We have this thing—believe me, it's an attractive thing and I like it. But I don't know if anything about you is even real."

God, he was right. Wade Hamilton was absolutely right. *He* didn't know her, but she'd kept tabs on him, researched him, knew a lot about him.

Not like a stalker or anything—or at least that was what she told herself. But every once in a while she'd see where he was or what he'd been working on. He did good work. He was a good man. The one-sided relationship she'd forged was the main reason she trusted him.

"What do you want to know?" she blurted into the darkness, unafraid of who might hear.

"They're probably listening," he reminded her. "Why not pass the time another way?"

His hand slid around her back, circling her waist, scooting her even closer to him. He didn't have to hit her over the head with the fact that he was attracted. But her real emotions got the best of her and crept through. She wanted a genuine relationship with him. Not a one-sided almost-stalker thing.

"There's no telling how long we'll be left here," she said, trying to play it cool. A real relationship. So that involved talking and not just necking as soon as they were alone. Right?

"To be honest, sitting in the dark next to you—practically naked like you are—isn't that bad." He put space between their hips. "It's not the worst situation I've ever been caught in. This doesn't make the top ten."

She bit back a laugh. "I don't know what possessed me to involve you."

"It's okay. Everybody panics occasionally." He rubbed the back of his neck, then his side.

"Not me."

"I'm not sure I believe you—" He slid a hand across her bare leg. "Instead of debating the ways people react to stress…why don't we just get back to what we can do in a dark room?"

Of all the sexy voices in the world, the owner of the one that affected her in the best way possible flirted with her. In a closet. In a dire situation where they may very well be killed. He bent his head and gave her a perfect kiss. Just enough pressure to suggest to her lips he didn't want to stop. But he did.

"I guess I deserve that after—"

His lips connected again. When they both were breathing extra fast he paused. "After all the teasing?"

"Teasing is what someone does who has no intention of following through," she pointed out.

Both of his strong arms wrapped around her and pulled her across his lap. "I have to say this is the most unusual date I've been on."

"Do you go on many?" She knew the answer.

After checking the bars for her, he sat on the same stool every Friday night for hours. She'd been so tempted to meet him there and talk. Deep down she'd known it would end like this. Okay, not necessarily sitting on a concrete floor as hostages. But definitely sitting on his lap...somewhere.

"I've been doing a lot of late night filing. It's kept me busy."

Huh? Oh, right, they'd been talking about his dating life. She let a nail wander across his collarbone and leaned forward to whisper in *his* ear.

"If we can't really do anything or make *plans*, let's get to know each other for real. Tell me one truth about yourself."

"Like...?"

"Your choice. It can be anything as long as it's the absolute truth," she continued whispering.

"Absolute?" he whispered back.

"No sugarcoating or stretching to make it fit first-date parameters."

He tapped her just above her heart. "Okay, but you go first."

"I hate alarm clocks."

"Doesn't count." He shook his head. "Everybody hates alarm clocks. Getting up in the morning isn't my favorite thing, either."

"Point taken." It had to be more intimate, something she wouldn't share with others. It had been so long since she shared something real. "I love running. Physical training. Give me a long path with no one else around and I'm in heaven. Your turn."

She tapped his knee next to her, afraid to glance directly at him and see an "are you serious?" look on his face. It hadn't been that intimate a gesture. His knee was covered with worn blue denim. Dragging her finger across his chest…*that* was intimate. Kissing him, sitting on his lap…intimate.

So why did she finally feel naked and vulnerable?

Dangerous territory.

She needed a distraction and fingered the strong black rope braided around Wade's left wrist, holding his watch. "I've always wondered about this strange watchband."

"Always?"

"You know what I mean."

She'd noticed it six weeks ago when he'd seen her at the FBI bust. But recognized it from when they'd first met. It wasn't the right time or place to remind him of that meeting. He'd definitely think she was a stalker. Shoot, she was having to convince herself she wasn't.

"I began wearing it again full-time after my capture last year. It's a little insurance policy. It might come in handy one day. Your turn."

"Oh no. It's still round one. That is definitely the same level as my alarm clock and totally not intimate."

"I have a better idea. Let's warm up a little."

One-handedly he unbuttoned the top two buttons of her borrowed shirt, causing her to shiver. Still sorting the emotion shooting through her, she forced herself to return to their lighthearted flirting. "So your motive is purely to get me warm?"

"Warm is good," he teased, winking before his lips captured hers again.

Kissing him was a little bit of heaven.

He behaved, keeping his hands in place, cupping her shoulder with his fingers to entice her to get closer. She tried to be careful not to sweep them up to the next level of desire—which would have been easy to do anywhere else. But he was quickly warming her inside and out. An unshaven cheek tickled a little before he abruptly brought his face away.

The bright light flooded the room when she opened her eyes. Wade quickly helped her to her feet and tucked her close to his side before walking through the hallway to meet Rushdan.

"Well, well, well." Rushdan smiled. "Welcome to the dark side, Ranger Wade." As he looked at their hands and snickered at Wade's obvious protectiveness.

"You came to a decision?" she asked, knowing the answer.

He splayed his hands and shrugged.

"Come on, Rushy, honey. If you intended to kill us, you would never have set eyes on us again." She turned to Wade. "He's sort of squeamish that way."

Wade cleared his throat, but his lips curved in the beginnings of a smile. "What do you want me to do?"

he asked, dropping both his head and his voice, then covering his face with his hand.

Rushdan might actually believe the whole pensive act. But that was all it was with Wade…just an act. He cleared his throat several times like he had after laughing himself into a coughing fit.

"Let's chat while Sal retrieves your first assignment." Rushdan placed his hand on Wade's shoulder.

The ranger stood taller, Rushdan's hand slid down and soon returned to his pocket. Wade continued to hold her hand. She yanked on it, hoping to remind him that Rushdan Reval was in charge. And that they wanted him to be.

If Wade continued to tower over the little fat man, it didn't matter what Wade *might* be able to do for him. When Wade didn't react, she squeezed a little harder and thrust her shoulder into his ribs.

"Rushdan, why not just tell us what you need us to do? Why all the drama and suspense?" she asked.

"Oh, allow me to have a little fun, darling Therese. And you should know by now I never discuss business with witnesses. Sal will inform you of where Texas Ranger man is going and what he'll need to do."

"You mean where *we're* going." She pointed to Wade and then herself. "I go where he goes. What do we need to do? And by when?"

"Today, my darling Therese."

"So it's last-minute, not well planned and no big deal if it goes wrong." She tapped one finger on the back of Wade's hand, hoping he got the message to let her go.

No luck. He squeezed her hand but didn't release it.

Finding and stopping the terrorists—her real assignment—was probably the most important thing she'd ever done. But keeping Wade alive ran a close second.

"Darling, this will be so easy for your boyfriend. It seems he has a very sordid past. At least in his youth. It's admirable that he turned his occupation around to work for him. Using his instinct and certain...skills." Her undercover employer stared again at their hands, fingers laced together.

"Do us all a favor, Rushdan, and stop talking in riddles. We already know Wade has a gambling problem."

"Yes, but do you know about his father?"

"Those records are sealed," Wade said, squeezing her hand tighter.

It was his cover. He didn't have to give her any sign. Had she worried about his ability to act before? Wade was a statue, stiff and unmoving. His eyes were hard like he wanted to rip Rushdan's head off.

"Dear, dear lover boy," Rushdan continued. "Everything can be found if you know how to look."

"I haven't run a game in years. I wouldn't know where to begin," Wade told him.

"Game?" she asked, trying to keep up.

"That's the beauty of today. It's waiting for you. All put together...just waiting." Rushdan clapped his hands together with excitement. "Give yourself credit. You know your way around a track. Who to look for. Where to look. This will be second nature for you."

"What's Rushdan talking about?" she asked, playing her part. "What records were sealed?"

"Mine. My childhood and teen years were filled by feeding my dad's gambling addiction." Wade rubbed his forehead with his free hand. "That is, until we were caught."

"You were in jail?" She heard the amazement in her voice. Not disappointment...more like wonder.

Why would she feel a kinship with him? They barely knew each other. Wait. They didn't know each other at all. And this was a perfect example. He was cute and had been helpful. And somehow she felt closer knowing he had more flaws than just following a hunch and jumping into situations.

Rushdan practically giggled like a girl. "Tell her all of it. Knock all the stars from her eyes."

It wouldn't help. She knew what Rushdan attempted to do. Crime boss Reval wouldn't ever make her his, no matter what she thought of Wade or what he shared from his past. She tucked herself closer into her ranger's side, more comfortable there by the minute.

She'd assumed Wade was an honorable man because of his occupation. But no modern Texas Ranger had been accused of something like this. They were the keepers of law.

"You look betrayed, my darling. Did you think

you were the first to lead this one—" he gestured as if dusting Wade's chest "—off the righteous path?"

Rushdan laughed, dabbing at the corner of his eyes as if tearing up.

"Aw, that's sweet. You were a delinquent, Wade." She rested her head on his arm. "How perfect. Where were you—"

"You've got more skills than I gave you credit," Wade said, finally dropping her hand, circling her waist instead. He hid the surprise of his past being revealed or kept a poker face for another reason.

Oh, Lord. She'd fallen for the fake background his partner had created. She should have known immediately that this man wouldn't have had a gambler for a father.

"That's enough reminiscing about sordid youths," Rushdan commanded. "We need this done quickly. Sal will give you the instructions and will be there to capture it all on video."

"Blackmail?" she asked.

"Insurance policy," Rushdan answered sharply.

"And Sal has all the details? Details that I had nothing to do with." She faced Rushdan straight on, keeping Wade's hand plastered across her stomach. "When are you going to accept me back?"

"If you weren't back, my darling, you wouldn't be in my building." Rushdan's voice held a menacing threat as he swept the bottom of her chin with his pointer finger. "Perk up, Ranger Wade. This should be old hat for you if you remember the racetrack. You do, don't you?"

Wade shrugged. She didn't know if that meant no, yes, or a big fat he-had-no-clue.

Rushdan sped up his short-legged steps and grabbed her upper arm as he began to pass, spinning her to face him. "This money is important, Therese. Don't screw it up." His anger literally spit through the gap in his front teeth.

Chapter Nine

Wade caught Therese as her "boss" thrust her away. Sal tried to grab her, but Wade stepped between them, blocking his reach. A leather bag hit the top of his boots.

"Everything's inside. Cash, names, bets and pay-offs." Sal didn't appear happy at the change of events. "Take the back exit." He glared at Wade before taking a long stare down Therese's robe. "You aren't decent enough for the front."

He drew his arm back ready to throw a punch but stopped himself. Therese stared at his chest, which quickly rose and fell as she tugged a little to get him headed in the right direction. He'd almost lost it from the disgusting look Reval's right-hand man had sent toward Therese.

Dressed like they'd gotten thrown out of a cheap hotel—no money of their own or phones—they watched Sal draw the door closed. "Remember we're watching the whole thing," Sal said through the thick steel.

"No ride?" Wade unzipped the bag, revealing

stacks of cash. "Do they expect us to walk to Lone Star Park?"

"We'll have a ride in a few minutes." She patted his chest with her palm.

Loving the feel of her hand sliding up and around his neck, he didn't wait for her to pull his lips down. He didn't mind kissing her at any time. But he did arch an eyebrow, questioning her timing.

"I could get used to this." He really could.

"You're so cute." She darted her eyes up and to the side of the building. He found the surveillance camera. Right. She was still acting.

"Cute? Not sure anyone's called me that since junior high." He winked and scooped up the bag of cash. "About that ride…"

"It'll require a little walking. At least it's eventually a sidewalk." She led the way out of the alley to a major street, then stepped into a large field.

"The building that looks like a bird's nest…that's the Irving Convention Center? Reval set up shop in Las Colinas. I hope you don't mind waiting a bit to get back to an open restaurant or fast-food joint."

"I think Sal will send a car. And if not, there's a hotel only ten minutes up the street." She pointed south toward the lake. "He's ultimately responsible for that bag you're carrying. I don't think he'll let us out of his sight for long."

To avoid parts of the dirt path, Therese jumped onto the curb occasionally. The late June sun hadn't heated the day completely but probably had made the pavement hot, so she couldn't use the street.

"You were pretty good back there," he said, shifting the bag to rest on his bare back. "Watch out for the broken beer bottles."

"Got it." She sidestepped onto the street, picking her feet up faster.

He could offer to carry her to the hotel, but he didn't think she'd go for it. She hadn't liked him throwing her over his shoulder last night.

He kept searching, but no cars were heading their direction—either from Reval's building or a Company B Ranger. He knew Jack or one of the men had followed them from the hotel. But they would keep out of sight until they were certain no one followed. That meant out of view from the building, leaving them a long walk.

Therese detoured into the street again, hopping from one foot to the other.

"Sure you don't want me to carry you?"

"Did you ask?" She shook her head. "But no thanks. Keeping the robe closed while I'm walking is a challenge. Besides, I think you explored my backside enough last night."

She laughed. He smiled, keeping an eye open for his team. It went without saying that they were close. Jack wouldn't have it any other way. So they were around here somewhere.

"Tell me about Reval." He needed to know more. "Not the paper version. What have you learned about him? Was today a normal reaction? Did he look desperate?"

"You want to know if he'd normally give us a bag

of cash?" She fast-walked a little down the street, avoiding more broken glass, rocks and trash.

"Exactly."

Another hundred yards and the apartments would block anyone watching from Reval's building. They hit the sidewalk and Therese winced, popping her feet up and down off the hot concrete. Wade scooped her up in his arms to get her under some shade a bit farther.

She kissed his cheek, not objecting to being carried. "Short answer...yes. Everything he's done in the past couple of days is within his character. And I promise you, Sal isn't far away. By now, he's in front of us somewhere, just waiting and watching."

"Like at the hotel."

"Probably." She locked her arms around his neck.

"Damn."

"Tell me what I'm missing, please."

Years of approaching vehicles as a highway patrolman had him searching between cars and behind the tiny things considered trees that they passed.

"Let's put the questions on hold a minute." He set her on the manicured grass of the apartment buildings along the road leading to the hotel. He pointed to the bag of money, shook his head, then covered her lips with his finger.

Therese pulled the robe tighter around her body, knelt and helped him look through the entire bag for a listening or tracking device. She also blocked their search from a couple of cars passing by.

"Looks like it's all clear. I'm pretty sure that Jack's at the hotel. At least, I would be there."

"How would he have known—" She put up a hand, realization plainly dawning on her face. "He followed us. That was risky. Why didn't you tell me?"

She lifted the gym bag and took off back to the main road. Wade caught her free arm, spinning her back to face him. The force caught her off balance and she fell into his chest. He slid the bag's strap off her shoulder and onto his own.

"It'll be okay. Trust me." He planted a quick kiss on her lips, receiving a small response. "My partners and I are good. Jack won't do anything to jeopardize putting Rushdan Reval back in jail. For good."

"I don't see Sal," she said.

"It doesn't mean you're wrong." He didn't miss that she hadn't said she trusted him.

Not a lot of vehicles went up and down the street, but he recognized one that pulled into the area reserved for those not staying long. Major Clements was one of the few Company B Rangers who actually drove a car instead of a truck.

He started toward the hotel entrance, but a strong tug on his arm pulled him in another direction.

"Maybe we shouldn't walk in through the *front* door?" Therese laced her fingers through his, heading across the street and into the hotel's parking garage.

She squeezed herself between the oak tree and hedge, waiting for him on the other side. He followed, stepped down from the retaining wall and into the coolness of the covered garage.

He lifted her down, not embarrassed that he drew her body close, wanting the athletic suppleness of her next to him as she slid to reach the concrete.

Her hands remained at his shoulders as she slightly tilted her gorgeous face up to his. "If we go to the lakeside, I think we can sneak over the fence and look like we're on our way to the hotel pool."

"Good idea."

They stayed put, not going where they needed to be. Not looking to see who was around or if anyone followed. It had been a long time since he'd stared into the eyes of a beautiful woman. An equally long time since he'd admired one so completely. Longer than both of those put together since he'd *wanted* to do either.

And whose fault was that?

"Not mine."

"Do all the ideas need to be yours?"

Dammit. The question had been so loud in his head that he'd answered out loud. "Nothing. We should probably get going."

The unbelievable sexual tension passed from his head but left his knees slightly wobbly. Right up to the point he heard the tires squealing on an upper garage floor.

"If it's Sal, we should just wait here."

"Not sure that's a great idea," he answered, securing the gym bag's shoulder strap across his body.

Therese stepped in front of him, stop-signing his

chest for him to quit or give up. "Even if your friends are inside, there's no way for us to explain how they might help us. Rushdan told Sal to give us a ride. He *is* coming and will expect us to be exactly like this, with no money, no cells and basically no clothing."

"And if he finds anything different, he'll be suspicious," he agreed.

"Basically he has permission to kill us and let Rushdan move forward with other plans."

"About those plans—" Wade saw movement out of the corner of his eye at the staircase. A silver-haired man resembling Major Clements.

"He hasn't told me a thing. That's why I risked following him last night," she said.

"Then it's agreed. We stay put and see who's about to drive around the corner any second." He raised his voice so his boss could hear, then tried to angle Therese behind him, but she wouldn't have it.

"I can take care of myself, Ranger."

"I've noticed that."

The car approaching from the upper floor could be a hotel patron, security, his partner or Reval's man, Sal.

"That's him," Therese said, stepping into the open. "Things just got a little bit easier."

Wade didn't have a chance to ask how.

Sal was already next to them, smoke curling from his open window. "Took you long enough. I ran out of cigarettes waiting on you."

"Then maybe you should have given us a ride at

Rushdan's office," Therese said before opening the door and scooting across the seat.

"You know I had to make sure your new boyfriend here wasn't being followed."

"And?" Therese asked.

Sal was silent as he inhaled his last drag on the butt, then threw it out the window.

"And nothing." Wade shoved the money bag between his feet. "Just like I said."

Sal drove too fast out the parking garage and away from the hotel.

At least nothing Sal could spot.

Major Clements dipped his head, hiding his face as they passed. Rushdan and Sal might recognize Jack and Slate, but the major was a different story. Today he looked like a faded old cowboy with a giant belt buckle and an old-fashioned snap shirt.

The tension between his shoulders eased at the knowledge the Rangers were there, trailing them, just out of sight.

"Take us to my apartment," Therese said as if Sal were her chauffer waiting for instructions.

"The boss said I need to—"

"Don't give any excuses, Sal. We all know I can't go to the track dressed in a robe. It's ridiculous to even suggest that Rushdan expects me to go like this." She tugged the hotel robe closed over her knee.

"What about him?" Sal asked. "You giving him back his shirt?"

"I can handle things after you drop us off."

"The boss ain't going to like that."

Wade listened to Therese handle Reval's right-hand man like she'd been ordering him around for years. Come to think about it, she probably had. So he stayed out of it and forced himself to look forward and not see if one of his friends followed.

Traffic was light early Saturday mornings. Sal turned off Northwest Highway and onto a side street soon after. He stopped at the corner, not bothering to take them to the gate. When Therese opened her door, Wade slid across the seat, following her, dragging the money bag with him.

Sal pulled away before the door closed.

Therese pulled the belt tighter and pushed the robe's collar higher on her neck. Wade stuck his head through the strap of the bag and shifted its bulk to his bare back.

"Lead the way. I'm starved. Your friends didn't provide breakfast."

"That's too bad. I don't cook, so I never go to the store." Therese kept a hand at her throat, holding the robe closed. She was actually more covered than she'd been in that yellow dress the night before.

"Not a problem. I know how to order pizza." It was sort of cute watching her be modest in case one of her apartment neighbors looked out their window.

"Pizza? For breakfast? Aren't we a little old for that?" She looked like she believed her words.

"We're not old and pizza delivers. Order the cinnamon breadsticks and it's like having those bite-size things you get at the airport. Shoot, it's too early for delivery. Maybe we could head to a restaurant?"

"I hate to disappoint you, but we don't have time to go out to eat. We have a lot of things to get done before we head out to the races." She passed by the pedestrian gate and crossed the drive toward the leasing office.

"If you're too old for pizza, we can still clean up and grab something. If I'm remembering correctly, there's a mom-and-pop diner back on Webb Chapel. They have terrific breakfast burritos they serve all day—" He grabbed her hand and turned her back to face him. "Isn't your apartment through there?"

"Yes—" Therese arched her eyebrows, waiting for him to catch on "—but I don't have my keys. I need management to unlock my door."

He tugged her toward the pedestrian gate. "Which apartment?"

She pointed to their left. "Twelve twenty-four. We should go to the office. I don't keep a key under the doormat. I don't even have a doormat."

"It'll be unlocked." He pulled her closer, kissing her quickly before she leaned back, trying to see their surroundings.

"Are you implying that one of your colleagues is waiting inside my apartment?"

"If we're lucky, there might even be breakfast. Then again…" He waggled his eyebrows at her while sliding his hands around her waist. "I might be luckier if there's not anyone around."

Chapter Ten

Was there time to get sidetracked? The gorgeous shirtless man caressing Therese around her waist sent an invitation with his eyes that she understood very well.

Wade made her forget about his implication that someone was inside her apartment. Her mind calculated how long they'd need to get ready and get to Lone Star Park. And then flooded with the disappointment that there would people expecting information. Or Sal demanding he escort them to the track.

Shoot! Wade's closeness was a problem…a huge distraction.

She turned the knob and walked inside without preparing herself defensively. Good grief, the door had been unlocked. They weren't alone. Just like Wade had said it would be. Her only thought had been…

Oh, God, she'd been hoping they'd have enough time to satisfy some of those teasing promises they'd been making.

Yeah, huge distraction.

"Did you bring something to eat?" Wade asked the man dressed in an apartment complex work shirt. They clearly knew each other and Wade had expected him to be here.

"No time."

"I was about to ask how you got in, but you must have picked up our things from the safe. Including my keys." Their phones sat on the coffee table along with her scuffed strappy shoes.

"Jack MacKinnon." He extended his hand and she took it. "I'm Wade's partner, mostly errand boy. At least to him."

"Therese Ortis, but you already know that. Normally my apartment is a little bit neater than this."

"Oh, yeah. I brought some of Wade's stuff and made it easy to find if someone checked you out. I also swept for bugs. You're clear, which I didn't think possible." He stuck electronic gear into a workman's bag, holding the straps in his hand.

"I see." She deliberately looked at the small suitcase and three pairs of men's shoes. Her small apartment was even smaller with both men standing in it.

Wade pulled open every cheap cabinet door in the small kitchen, looking inside. "Man, Therese. You really don't have any food here. Not even peanut butter. Who doesn't have peanut butter?"

Jack reached into the bag and brought out two weapons. He set them on the kitchen bar and tried to look casual, leaning against the wall. "Brother, I'm not going to tell you what we've gone through to make this operation happen and cover your you-know-what. After this one's finished, we're going to have a little talk."

"I figured Major Clements would be talking the loudest. I didn't really have a choice. The opportunity happened." His eyes cut to her and back to the fridge. "Once you guys discovered who and what we were dealing with…did you have a problem?" Wade stared into the freezer. "Man alive. There's not even any frozen dinners or ice?"

"Sorry to say you have some very bad friends, ma'am," Jack said, shaking his head at Wade. "Come on, man, contribute to the conversation."

"What?" Wade shrugged and let the freezer shut.

Therese answered with a shrug and mouthed, "I told you so."

"We probably don't have much time," Jack continued. "Slate is keeping an eye on Rushdan's man who dropped you off." He looked at his phone as if expecting an update. "After dropping you, he went to a 7-Eleven. I think the team is getting up to speed on the situation. Anything happen after we spoke last night? That is, anything I should know?"

"The bag I brought in is full of cash and we're due at Lone Star Park as soon as possible," Wade threw out casually. "A lot of cash that Rushdan Reval wants to increase."

"So I guess you don't need any cash. Your truck's back at your place. If anyone was watching it, we had it towed."

Wade gave a few more details but left out how

he'd been used as a punching bag or how she'd tried to leave him in the truck.

"Did you set up the phone to listen in?" Wade asked.

"Yours, yes. The FBI had a few dozen choice words when we tried Miss Ortis's. Yours should be enough to keep tabs on you." Jack pointed to their phones at the end of the kitchen bar.

Wade's partner lifted his cell phone from his back pocket and read a message. "Gotta run. You've got company coming."

Then Texas Ranger Jack MacKinnon slid open the patio door and hopped over the four-foot patio fence with grace.

He'd cut it close.

Sal barely knocked, turned the knob and came inside. "Boss sent me for a walk-through. Believe me, this ain't my idea."

Rushdan's man picked up a pair of slacks from the back of the couch, dropping them immediately. He went as far as to look inside the bathroom cabinet, finding a slightly used toothbrush that didn't belong to her. Their weapons along with a Texas Rangers badge were on the two-person dining table.

"You shouldn't leave those just lying around anywhere," he said, pointing to the credentials and weapons. "You don't know who's going to sneak inside and lift stuff." When he was satisfied, he tossed an envelope in Wade's direction and left, slamming the door.

"Well, that was interesting," Wade said, dropping onto her couch the minute the door closed.

Therese turned the two bolts she'd installed herself, locking everyone out. She wasn't used to anyone being in the small apartment. No one had ever been there other than a maintenance man.

And yet, having Wade there didn't feel strange or awkward.

No distractions. And no thoughts of them together. They had work to do.

She scooped up his clothes, draping them over the end of the couch before reaching for the envelope. But Wade gently tugged on her hand, pulling her onto his lap.

"Don't you think we should open that?" she asked before glancing at the clock radio on the kitchen bar.

He skimmed the side of her knee with one large hand. And kept the envelope behind her back. He pulled her close enough to kiss her neck.

"Maybe you should read what's inside the envelope before we get sidetracked?" she asked while he nibbled.

"You don't think it's the same instructions that are in with the money?" He dropped the sealed brown envelope onto her lap but didn't relinquish his hold.

"I've never done anything like this for Rushdan before, so I really don't know." She ripped the edge open, then slid her finger, opening up the long side. She tipped it up and a cheap cell phone along with a piece of paper fell to her lap. "Maybe I should sit—"

"We can read it together if you stay where you are. Unless you don't feel comfortable?"

"I'm plenty comfortable. Too comfortable." Her

arm brushed the bare skin of his chest, sending her stomach flipping wildly. She got up quickly before she could change her mind about getting even more comfortable.

There would be plenty of time to get to know Wade better. Plenty of time when they weren't due at the racetrack. She flipped the one typewritten page open, holding it by the corner just in case there were fingerprints to process.

"I don't know why I'm being careful. Rushdan doesn't run his *business* with any connections to himself. It's the reason he's out of jail, rebuilding his empire. Lots of non-prosecutable people do the dirty work."

"His cronies don't know what they're writing or what piece of the puzzle they might be acting on. We discovered that last year after he tried to kill me."

"Rushdan is the only person who has an inkling what the whole picture looks like." She stood by the sliding door, searching the edges of buildings to see if anyone lurked about.

"What's it say?" Wade asked.

"These instructions are different than those in the money bag," she said, handing the note to him as he joined her. "Everything he's done so far is part of a test to see where we'd go or who we'd call."

"And who stopped to help," he pointed out, tugging her to the couch again. He flipped the paper to the side table. "Seems awful risky to be switching the plans around from us placing bets to being the ones who pay out the bribes—at least in this version. Damn risky."

"I should grab a quick shower and get some real clothes on. Unless you want to go first?" She stood, tossed the cheap cell phone with the others and tried to pass by Wade. He didn't let her.

He tugged a little on her hand—too gently for her to blame him for keeping her there.

He shook his head. "I want a kiss." He guided her back to his lap, then placed a fingertip under her chin, drawing her lips to his.

The kiss was good, fulfilling, sexy. Long enough for him to maneuver his hands behind her back and press her breasts against his strong chest. More than enough to shoot her senses into overdrive. More than enough for her to potentially forget why they needed to be anywhere else.

Feeling safe within his arms, she found it hard to ease away. Especially when she wanted more of him. Her longing was getting harder and harder to control. And why was she thinking about feeling safe?

Safety wasn't one of her priorities. Putting Reval in prison for good, discovering who the cash was behind Public Exposure and getting the algorithm off the streets—those were her priorities.

Three things that would make a lot of people safe.

She scooted off his lap, pulled his shirt down around her thighs and tightened the sash around her waist. "We can take my car unless you think that's a bad idea. Jack said your truck was at your place. Is it far?"

Liar! It wasn't far at all. About three miles. She'd known exactly where he lived when she'd agreed to rent this place. Being alone, working alone like she had been for so long isolated her. Getting an apartment close to someone she knew—okay, knew of— was her one gift to herself.

She'd given up a lot to work with Homeland. Her parents may have died when she was eighteen, but she had lots of family in the San Antonio area. Tons of relatives who all thought she'd cheated on a test while at the police academy and had been kicked out. Several knew she worked with a small-time crime boss. Not that she worked for the FBI on loan to the Department of Homeland Security.

Shoot. Wade didn't even know that part.

Wade's steel blue eyes searched hers. "Thinking of something you need to tell me? Another truth-or-dare question?"

"I don't remember any dares." She shook her head. "I thought we were getting to know each other."

He tugged on the long lapels of the hotel robe until her hands were supporting her weight, split on either side of his face against the couch. It brought their lips close. So close she could feel him move to form his next words.

"There's another way for us to get to know each other better," he whispered against her lips.

"Do you…ah…want a shower?"

"You go ahead, I need some air." He took a deep breath and exaggeratedly shifted his seating position.

After that kiss, she needed some air, too. She ran

to the bathroom, throwing her back against the door to save herself.

Pure oxygen might help clear her head. She opened the bathroom window and overheard Wade. He was on the small patio, talking into his phone. She had a sneaking suspicion he didn't need *air* as much as a discussion with his fellow Rangers.

So why not just tell her that?

Because he didn't trust her. Not completely.

She gently shut the window to give him his privacy, twisted the lock and began the shower. This time he couldn't "accidentally" open the door and see her in her birthday suit. A girl should leave some mystery. She hadn't last night, but Ranger Wade Hamilton still remained a gentleman. A teasing gentleman, but a gentleman just the same.

After the past two years of being in his life but not being *in* his life… Well, she'd given him no reason to trust her at all. How could she blame him for being hesitant?

The opportunity to come clean, to tell him *why* she trusted him had come and gone. Maybe they would continue the game about getting to know each other. But what if it was just a game for him?

She rinsed out her hair and dropped her forehead to the tile, letting the stream of water pound the back of her neck. It wasn't really sore, she just needed to think. Or think about another subject that wasn't Wade.

They should both be dead.

What was Rushdan Reval really up to? Why did

he need Wade for his plans? He wasn't the sort of guy who easily forgave anyone. Everything he did had a selfish reason attached to it. Everything.

For weeks he'd had his people searching for someone with access to public facilities. Rushdan had never hinted that it had anything to do with Public Exposure. But the speed at which he'd acted today made her think it did.

Wade would help her find out why the domestic terrorism group wanted the algorithm and how it had been improved or upgraded. He was her way inside Rushdan's inner circle. Wade. Again unknowingly playing the part of her hero. But no longer in the teenage-crush way she'd fantasized about for too long.

No, this was worse. He was a nice guy. A considerate person. A competent lawman. Distracting. She could actually fall for the real person she'd discovered him to be.

Chapter Eleven

Wade awoke from the nudge Therese gave him as they exited the highway close to the racetrack. He hadn't slept—or napped—long, but it had been deep and reviving. Something he'd needed after staying awake most of the previous night.

"I think I'm getting too old for hands-on law work," he said.

"Why's that?"

"Maybe too many days behind my desk recently." He stretched and yawned. "I could have stayed up two nights in a row back in my highway patrol days."

Therese looked sort of funny, paused like she was about to speak, and then she looked out her window. What had he missed?

She hadn't complained when he suggested a nap. In fact, she'd told him to close his eyes. He didn't regret it. There was no telling when he'd get the real thing again and he needed to be on his toes.

A long line of cars was turning into Lone Star Park and it was almost ten o'clock. They were running a few minutes behind but it shouldn't be a big deal. She hadn't seemed anxious in any of the life-threatening situations they'd been in before.

He couldn't pin it down. Was she thinking about Reval's elusive comment about his past? Was she catching on? Would it change her opinion if she knew that he'd run scams like this for real until he was fifteen?

"Will it be easy to find the guy the instructions told us to find? Do you think he'll leave if we're a couple of minutes late? I could drop you off and park the car alone if it will save time." Therese tapped her thumbs against the steering wheel, waiting on the light to turn green.

"Are you nervous or something?" he asked, hoping it didn't really have anything to do with his youth.

"I guess. Aren't you? We didn't really talk about what we were going to do to find the guy, bribe him or even get the money inside the park." She paused for traffic and looked at him. "I mean, that's an awful lot of money in that bag. Who pays off a bribe with cash at the actual race track? Our odds of succeeding are not high."

"Trust me. It'll go fine." He shook his head, but some weird business was happening with his stomach. It had nothing to do with pulling off the bribe. He'd taken care of that with a phone call while Therese had showered.

He didn't have to think too hard about what caused his anxiety. It had been in the background since hearing Reval's words that morning. Having the crook tell him to come to the track had his insides bobbing around like a cork on a fishing line.

Every distraction he'd tried at the apartment had been countered by Therese. There had been a new professionalism in her since she'd showered. He'd ordered food while she dried her hair. They ate in separate rooms and hadn't really talked since he'd fallen asleep soon after getting in her car.

Therese signaled and turned into the racing complex, reading all the signs aloud. He pointed to the left lane away from the regular parking area. It was pretty obvious she'd never been to the races before. But he had. A major portion of his misspent youth had been running behind those gates.

But after he'd returned to Dallas as a ranger, he'd avoided setting foot in the place. No concerts. No nights out with the guys. No Triple-A ballgames at the stadium next door. No cases associated with anything to do with racing or betting.

Hell, he didn't even allow himself to drive on the frontage road around the entertainment complex. He'd done pretty good not looking back for his entire adult life. But now...

Now it rushed him like speeding down the hill of the Titan at Six Flags. Riding a roller coaster wasn't something he'd done since he was a kid, either. He had to control the sickening anticipation of what needed to be done. He had to rein it in, use it to his advantage.

This wasn't a theme park with a fake shoot-out in the Wild West. If he screwed up...

He rolled his shoulders—stretching, relaxing, shaking off the nerves. He wouldn't screw up. He wouldn't let Therese down. He wrestled the fifteen-year-old's memories back behind that locked door in his mind.

Therese pulled behind a line of cars for the parking lot. He remembered exactly where he needed to go for the bribes and broke out of his funk. He put a hand on Therese's shoulder, then pointed for her to head straight.

"Keep heading down this road. Enter through the owner/trainer gate. Then we get to the stables and jockey quarters without any real questions."

"Are you sure, the note said to—"

"What if that's just another test? Look, Therese. I've forgotten more about this track than other people can possibly discover. Trust me. If you want to drop off a bribe, you don't take it through the front gate."

"Forgotten? You've done this before?"

She passed the patron parking lots and main entrance of the park, continuing around the curve to an entrance he remembered all too well.

"What do I tell Sal?" she asked.

"Maybe exactly what I just told you. Or you just let me handle it."

She pulled over, parking just inside, next to the fence. The cell given to them in the envelope rang. Wade pressed the speaker button so Therese could hear.

"Where are you?" Sal yelled.

"We're doing what you instructed," she answered before he could open his mouth.

"I'm supposed to be with you," Sal complained.

"Bribing a jockey is going to be a little conspicuous if someone's on our tail with their phone pointed in our direction." Wade covered her hand when she reached for the cell. "We'll catch up with you after we're done."

He clicked the phone off while Therese tried to swipe it from him.

"I'm not sure that was such a great idea," she said.

"Trust me. We'd be arrested within a couple of minutes his way. Come on, let's get this over with."

They might be arrested any way they tried to pull this off. He reached over the seat, grabbed the bag of money and slid out the door. He kept walking. Not waiting on Therese. Not turning around to see if she even followed.

The car lock and beep of her horn told him he could keep striding between the trucks and trailers. But all of a sudden he doubled over, unable to catch his breath.

"Wade? Are you okay? What happened?"

Therese's questions swam through his head. He heard them but something kept him from answering. He stood straight, catching the end of a horse trailer before he fell over a second time.

"Oh my God, what's wrong with you?" Therese rubbed his back and gripped his upper arm so tight it just might have held him up.

What's wrong? Images swam in front of his eyes,

obliterating the real parking lot in front of him. Years drifted away and he was a lanky teenager with his hair hanging in his eyes, jeans he barely kept around his hips and a T-shirt that was sure to have some foul writing.

"I'm…uh…not sure." But he knew. He was having a flashback.

"If you can't—"

"I can. I'm okay." He pushed himself to his full height again as he shoved the thoughts of his father's arrest back to the place they'd been locked before.

They didn't stay. But he couldn't allow those memories to interfere with today. Everything he saw, smelled…hell, even the sizzle of excitement was like stepping back in time. He was fifteen again and throwing up while they cuffed his father and hauled him to jail.

It was the last time he'd seen his father before the trials. The first one had convicted his dad of everything from petty larceny to organized crime. His father never made eye contact during the second trial for child endangerment. Terrence Hamilton had given up his paternal rights and Wade had never seen him again.

"Never look back," he heard himself mumble his father's mantra.

"What? Wade, you've got to clue me in on what's going on." She stopped him from stepping around her by a gentle touch to his chest.

He could see where he needed to go, knew what he needed to do. It was all right there if he kept looking over her head. She softly cupped his cheek and his knees shook.

"We're going to be late," he squeaked out.

"Better late than dead."

"Everything's okay, Therese. I won't let you down." Dammit, she caught his gaze and locked eyes with him.

It felt like she could see through his lies. Her X-ray vision into his soul made her eyes crinkle around the corners. The hand she had on his chest slid to his belt loop and shook him while she released an exasperated "errr."

"You're a very frustrating man. What did you mean when you said you'd forgotten more about this place than others could discover?"

If another woman had been in front of him, he wasn't certain what he would have done. But their get-to-know-each-other game of truthful facts tugged at him to tell her everything, to not hold back.

"I know my way around."

"You didn't have a real gambling problem. Did you?"

"No. Do you think I'd be a ranger— Hell, I'd be out of a job so fast."

"Then what is it?"

His hands found their way to each side of her waist. He was about to physically move her out of his path. But he looked into her eyes and realized his breathing was normal. His knees were rock steady.

The formidable memories of witnessing his father's arrest faded as he looked at a beautiful dark-haired woman. Dressed in lots of...sequins? He hadn't noticed until the sunlight bounced off a couple, making him blink back to reality.

"We need to get moving. Remember that whole thing about our real objective?"

"Hard for me to forget after three years." She stepped aside so they could continue. "You sure you're all right?"

"One of those punches caught up with me, that's all. A momentary thing."

The opportunity to come clean passed by without a second thought. Okay, so he was thinking about it as they walked between the vehicles. It wasn't a big deal. No one in his current world would care.

The guys would slap him on the back and might ask a question or two. He'd proven himself to Company B. He belonged there. They already knew he had their backs and was willing to put himself at risk.

But did Therese? Did she know?

More important, would *she* still trust him or think he'd been lying?

Just say it, man!

"This is probably going to sound funny." Therese laced her fingers through his. "I heard if you want a sure way to tell which horse will win the race, you should watch them before they're saddled. Then bet on the last one that went pee."

"Where the hell did you hear that crock?" He laughed.

She laughed. "My dentist. It's exactly what he does."

"And it works?"

"He swears by it."

"In my experience there's only one sure way that a horse wins." He patted the bag of money. "Bribery."

Chapter Twelve

Not many people gave them a second look as they walked between the buildings housing the horses, jockeys and owners. Therese looked everywhere, taking it in, still hyperaware that Sal could be around any corner. Sal or the police. Getting arrested would blow everything.

She also watched Wade. He didn't seem sick and didn't act like getting punched in the gut hours ago had anything to do with what had happened in the parking lot. Honestly, it seemed like he'd seen a ghost.

She wasn't used to seeing strong men like him stumble. One minute he stood tall and the next he was practically on the ground.

"Any idea where to find this guy we're supposed to pay off?" she whispered.

Wade pointed to a stall where an older cowboy tightened a buckle on a saddle.

"Are you sure? He looks too...tall." Wade arched both of his brows, waiting for her to explain. So she continued in a whisper, "I thought we'd be paying off the jockey like the instructions say."

"We'd be caught faster than any of these horses can run. The jockeys are watched a lot closer than the stable hands. We slip this guy the money, then he'll slip a jigger into the race."

"I have no idea what you just said." He tried to step around her, but she moved in front of him. She needed an answer. "He's also not the man Rushdan wants us to contact. Why not just do things his way?"

"A jigger is kind of like a small cattle prod they use to get extra speed at the last minute." His confidence looked to be back. "This is something I know, Therese. Trust me."

Wade took a step forward again, but she latched on to his arm to stop him. *Trust him?* Everything she'd sacrificed clawed its way to the surface from somewhere deep down where it had been buried for years.

Fear. Apprehension. Doubt. Especially doubt...

The self-assured character she presented to the world shrank back, giving way to the lonely undercover agent. The real her sat alone way too often, questioning every move she made.

What in the world was wrong with her? She'd never hesitated as much as in the past twenty-four hours.

"Oh sssugar!"

Yeah, she'd said it loud enough for everyone around them to hear. She got a confused expression from Wade and had startled the man he'd been watching. The stall cleaner's face changed from surprise to recognition when he concentrated on Wade.

"Well, I'll be a horse's patootie. As I live and breathe. Is that you, Wade? You've kind of filled out." He carefully tipped the pitchfork behind him and spread his arms wide.

"It has been fifteen years, Joey. I remember you as older." Wade walked into the old man's embrace.

"True. Every word, true."

Therese watched in silence and wonder. Wade Hamilton had a past. A real one with...regular people. People who matched the sealed files Rushdan had discovered. The Rangers hadn't built this background. It was real. Wade Hamilton had a sealed juvie record. The fact sort of stunned her. No wonder he'd laughed so hard when she'd said they'd known each other.

"Who's your friend?" Joey asked as the two men separated.

"This is Therese."

She stepped forward to shake his hand but he held it up to stop her.

"Mind your step, Miss Therese. Maybe I should come your direction."

Therese mumbled a "nice to meet you" and stayed put just inside the stall's entrance. But as Joey took a step, her new partner reached in front of him, grabbing the pitchfork.

"We should stand over here, out of sight." He quickly moved the horse poo to the far wall, making room for them.

There was a story there. Some bond between the two men that she really wanted to understand. It was a story for another time. Joey was more than just Wade's friend. But her curiosity would have to wait.

"You in trouble again?"

"No, sir, but I have a favor that might bring some your way."

"I heard you'd gotten out of the game, gone straight, were making something of yourself."

There was suddenly a great deal of tension charging the musky air. She sensed Wade respected the older man and wanted to be straight with him. His jaw muscles visibly flexed. But he knew they couldn't. It would put everything at risk…including Joey.

Someone out there had an algorithm that could potentially harm thousands. The organizers they'd caught from the domestic terrorist group Public Exposure had promised a catastrophe would happen in Dallas. That specific threat had been thwarted by capturing the group's FBI contact six weeks ago. Only a copy of the program had been found…not the original or the person who had developed it.

The programmer put the algorithm on the market again. Rushdan Reval was facilitating a new sale to the highest bidder. He claimed this version was more destructive than the original.

If Wade couldn't guarantee a win for one of these races Rushdan wouldn't get the cash he needed to proceed. Or he wouldn't have the leverage he wanted to include Wade in the plan.

Then they'd be back to square one.

"I wish I could explain, sir."

The older man shook his head.

"It's a matter of life and death." She heard the words fly from her lips.

Joey's eyes grew big and round in his weathered face. He shifted from foot to foot, clearly conflicted about lending aid.

She moved closer and took Joey's hand between hers. "Wade says you're the one who can help, I know you can. You probably think I'm exaggerating. I mean, life and death, who even says that? You have absolutely no reason to trust me. Please help us."

God, she hoped he would.

They needed a break.

"I suppose that's a lot of cash in that bag," Joey said.

Wade nodded.

"I hate to ask—"

"To tell the truth I had high hopes for you, son. I thought that lawman straightened you out. I've been on a narrow path of redemption for a while myself."

"This is a bad idea," Wade said flatly.

"I won't tell you the thought hasn't crossed my mind once or twice. Make a killin' and retire on some island paradise. I wouldn't go up against the real mobsters out here. Look at what happened to your old man."

"You're right. It's too dangerous," Wade said. "I don't know what I was thinking. Forget it."

Therese watched the genuine emotion on both

men's faces. The admiration, then sadness in Wade's eyes. The disappointment in Joey's. She wanted to jump in and tell Joey about the good man Wade had become.

Had she been worried about Wade's ability to keep their objective secret? He was about to let this man think the worst possible things about him.

She pressed herself into the stable wall covering her mouth with her hand. It was the only way she could keep herself from blurting out the real reason they were there.

"Well, I can't rightly do that," Joey pushed his hat off his forehead and smiled. "Thankfully, no one will be expecting me to rig anything."

He walked to the stall door and stuck his head out, looking both directions.

"You'll help us?" she asked, surprised by the man's agreement.

"Rightly so, little lady. I should have helped this boy when he was twelve and didn't. No way am I standing around like a wallflower again." He shut the door behind him as he spoke, enclosing them in the tight space. He sniffed a little—not at the smell but wiped away the sign of a tear—before cupping Wade's shoulder in a manly acknowledgment.

Joey claimed to be an upstanding citizen, but he knew exactly which jockey or horse owner was open to accepting a bribe. In a few short sentences he laid it all out for Wade. It was a shorthand she couldn't completely follow, but something Wade had no problem deciphering.

After accepting a couple of stacks of the cash to bribe the jockey, Joey pushed them both out of the stall.

"I'll send note when everything's set. You know it'll be best if I disappear for a while 'til things are cleared up."

"Take this," Wade said trying to give Joey another stack of cash.

"No thanks. Favors don't come with price tags. Come back around when all the dust settles. Don't be a stranger." He patted them both on the back before he swaggered bowlegged past the other open stalls.

Wade took her hand in his and led them in the opposite direction.

"That's it?"

"Yeah. Well, we still have to place some bets. And I know right where to find the people we need."

"I bet you do." She had a long stride, but she practically ran to keep up with Wade. "You weren't kidding when you said you've done this before. If I didn't know better, I'd say you have real-life experience as a gambler. You have the lingo down perfect. No wonder they established your background so quickly."

Was that what Rushdan had been hinting at? Did Wade have some sort of juvie record? Joey had spoken of letting Wade down when he was twelve.

"Therese, if we had more time I'd explain. But we don't."

"I know. I know. I'll have to *trust* you."

Her words didn't get any reaction. They reached

a corner close to where the crowds clamored around and he dropped the bag on her shoulder.

"Stay back where those two hallways meet, out of the line of cameras. I'll be sending several people to you. They'll all say I did. You give them a couple of grand each."

"Tell me one thing that's personal—and relevant—and I promise not to bombard you with questions of how this is possibly going to work."

She swore his eyes rolled as he tipped his white felt hat to the crown of his head.

"One thing." He held up his index finger before leaning in close next to her ear. "It's true. My father was a gambler and con artist. He was in jail several years and I put him there when I was fifteen."

He pivoted and hurried away before she could draw breath to whisper, "Wow."

The bundles of cash weren't in stacks of thousands, so she darted into the closest family restroom and locked the door. She counted quickly, not allowing herself to think about a fifteen-year-old Wade turning his father in to the police.

Of course she thought about it. But she got the money ready and took her place to wait. Several minutes passed before the first person stood next to her against the wall and said, "Wade sent me."

Nine men and women stopped next to her and inconspicuously flattened their palm to collect the money just out of view of the cameras monitoring everything. She gave it to them without questions or even direct eye contact.

"Well, lookie here." Sal stepped from around the corner. "You're finally showing up and you still got the money? What the hell are you playing at? You're going to get us both killed."

He reached for the almost empty bag but she twisted the strap around her wrist. If he pulled at it, he'd make a scene.

"We've got it under control." Her calm, confident voice didn't reflect her jumping insides. She tried to see past Sal but he blocked her view of the main area where Wade and the people he'd been sending were located.

Sal turned quickly, pinning her to the wall, his finger poking deep into the fleshy part of her shoulder.

"I've never understood why the boss keeps you around. You ain't smarter than any of the rest of us. Just remember that this cop's severed head rests on your shoulders. Totally your fault when he disappears."

She let him poke her. Let him push her back into the wall until her bare skin pinched. Let him get in her face without loosening her grip on the bag. She stood firm, raising her chin a little more defiantly while staring into his watery, sad eyes and smelling his bad breath.

Whatever doubt had been tugging at her brain had fled. She was once again in the moment and remembering that she *had* done this job alone for a very long time. Wade might have the upper hand on fixing a horse race but she could navigate Rushdan's men.

An arm dropped across Sal's shoulders. He immediately stepped back but he couldn't free himself from Wade's embrace.

"Funny seeing you here, Sal. Checking up on us?"

Sal ducked his head, slipping from Wade's grip. "Man, you don't know who you're messin' with!"

"Calm down, Sal." Wade shifted his weight, draping his arm around her shoulders. "Babe, this is my buddy, Dale Beauchamp. He'll be taking that bag off our hands. Don't worry. He also placed our bet for us."

She didn't want to give Sal any reason to report to Rushdan that something was wrong. She swallowed her nerves—the ones that increased her breathing each time Wade stood next to her.

The strap of the bag slid off her shoulder and into the hands of a good-looking man about the same build and age as Wade. If he was from her partner's time here as a child she couldn't tell. More likely he was another part of the rangers' plan that she didn't know.

Dale eased the bag from her, holding the handle as he smiled and winked. "See you 'round, Hamilton."

Sal took a step in the same direction. Just one step before Wade slammed his palm into his chest, stopping him cold.

"You should hang around for the fun, Sal. Winning big calls for a celebration."

"You better win big, Hamilton. The boss expects his investment to mature. Keep the phone. Someone will be in touch." Sal walked away, obviously searching for the direction Dale Beauchamp had gone with the cash before lifting his hand to hide his face from the cameras.

Therese couldn't believe so much had happened in such a short time. Whatever respect she'd held for the Texas Rangers before, it didn't compare to how high she held them now.

They worked fast. About as fast as she was falling for the strong man beside her.

Chapter Thirteen

Wade saw the security guard passing to Sal's right. He remembered the old familiar rush, felt the adrenaline surge through him again.

"Well, that was easy," Therese said, heading toward the track.

Wade stood there a moment, tamping down the shakiness in his arms and legs. He snapped a picture of Dale walking away, fingers gripped around the bag handle. No one was taking the rest of the money from that Texas Ranger.

How many times had Wade been the handoff, receiving his father's payoff. Or more accurately the winnings of whatever group his dad was fronting for. Wade should make certain Therese understood the truth. He'd confessed haphazardly. He made this operation seem easy because it was second nature to him.

Still. Even after all this time.

Calling upon that cocky kid who carried around thousands of dollars, afraid of nothing, had been too easy.

"Wade? Are you coming? Do we get to watch which horse wins? I mean...we *are* here." Therese asked.

"Sure."

She waited until he stood beside her again. Lacing her fingers through his, she smiled at him as they headed through the crowd, back to the track's rail. They looked like any other couple betting a few bucks on a few horse races. He didn't have to work at keeping her close to his side. He wanted her there.

Dammit. Why had he allowed being here to hit him so hard? He'd controlled the emotions associated with this part of his life for years.

For a couple of panicked minutes he'd actually become that lost fifteen-year-old kid. But he didn't care about the old man who'd taught him to steal and cheat. He didn't. Terrence hadn't been a father to him.

Fred Snell was the only real man who had taken on that role.

Therese tugged on his arm. "Are you feeling sick again? You're looking sort of sick."

He shook his head, dropping his hand on top of hers, gathering warmth for his icy fingers. "I'm good."

"This is so exciting. Even if I know one jockey is—" she dropped her voice so only he could hear through the crowd noise "—you know, going to do whatever to win."

They stood through a couple of races. Each time his sequined companion would turn her face to his and he'd ask her who she'd thought would win. She actually chose one who placed, but not the winner. Then it was time. She asked. He nodded.

Therese didn't need to know specific details. Didn't need to know that the one wearing purple dot silks would send a shock through his horse at the last minute to make it run faster.

The crowd was happy and unworried, waiting for the start of the race as the horses lined up in the gate. The boards reflected great—but not too great—odds for Texas T.

The gates opened and hooves pounded the ground, dirt flew and muscles rippled through the beautiful horseflesh of each mount. Memories of other races rushed through his mind, keeping him silent. Back then he hadn't wanted to draw attention to himself.

Authorities questioned the race when they'd seen him or his father or his father's cronies. It was one of the reasons he'd been so active in delivering money and messages when he was younger, smaller. Then overnight he'd grown tall enough to be spotted.

Then caught.

Therese waved her fingers in front of his nose. "Hey, did we win?"

Damn, it was over? He looked at the board and verified the race results. "Reval will get his money."

"So we're done? I'm sort of confused how we're going to collect the winnings since we didn't place the bets."

"Right." He glanced around. "I don't see anyone

watching us, but it's probably better to have this conversation when no one can overhear."

They'd barely closed the car doors when the phone Sal gave them buzzed inside his back pocket. He pushed the speaker button in time to hear "Money. Mustangs. Las Colinas Boulevard. One hour."

"That's not going to happen. It'll take my guy twenty-four hours to get the cash together for that sum." For the Rangers or Homeland or some other government bureaucracy.

"That wasn't what you were supposed to do," Sal screamed.

"Oh yeah? Neither was going to jail, which is what would have happened if I'd bet that much cash. But that was the real test, right?"

"What?" Therese mouthed.

He waved her off, pointing to the phone. Waiting for a response from Reval's crony.

"Keep the phone handy. The boss will be in touch." The call blinked with a disconnection.

Eyes forward, Therese started the engine, put the car in gear and spun the tires a little as she pulled from the lot full of horse trailers and trucks. He'd read about people's knuckles turning white as they gripped the steering wheel. Therese had a death grip on the plastic and it was hard to miss.

She also wove in and out of traffic like a racing pro. Otherwise anyone watching wouldn't be able to tell she was upset. Her expression was…expressionless. The beautiful smile he'd grown accustomed to in such a short time in just twenty-four hours…

That smile hadn't been there since they'd gotten inside the car.

They seemed to be headed toward her apartment when the route changed, and two turns later they were close to his house. How did she know where he lived? A few minutes later, screeching to a halt, she threw the car into Park and smashed the door unlock button.

"I take it that's my cue," he opened the door, still wondering what he'd said or hadn't said as he stepped out.

"Wade?"

"Therese," he said, leaning to look inside.

She held her palm out and gestured for him to hand something over. "Leave the phone."

"We're not waiting together? Inside?"

She flipped her fingers again and he complied, handing over the phone.

"I'll be in touch." She revved the engine, waiting.

"Dammit, Therese. What did I do?" Had he pushed the "I know what I'm doing bit" too far? He could concede that he had. He'd tell her that if he knew they weren't being watched. Watched by either side—Reval's men or the rangers. "Come on inside and I'll explain."

"Don't try to smooth this over by throwing me your all-innocent look. It sounds petty when I say this is my operation. But dammit, Wade, it is. You can't unilaterally make decisions and think I'm okay with it. I'm not. My supervisors won't be. This is way too complicated. There's more at risk than just bringing Rushdan Reval to his knees."

THERESE WANTED TO peel out. Wanted to leave him standing curbside with that complete look of bewilderment on his face. But she couldn't. He'd made sure that they were tied together waiting for the operation's next move.

"You seriously don't get it?"

"What?" he asked, shrugging his sturdy shoulders up into his neck. "Come inside and let's…talk."

Right. Like talking was what he'd want to do if they were alone. Sure, she wanted answers. More than just one at a time from their little game. But more important, she had to make him understand how critical this assignment was. Its completion was her way back. Back to a normal life. Back to friends. Back home.

"We could continue the Q and A you began this morning. The place is clean. No bugs—at least electronic ones—so, it's safe to talk," he said in a persuasive tone. But he didn't look too thrilled about another round of talking. He shut the car door and ambled across his lawn anyway. Yeah, she'd just thought he "ambled" across his lawn.

Must be his boots.

Wade wasn't like any man she'd dealt with. Granted, most of the men in her adult life had been criminals—were criminals. Then again, it turned out Wade had been, too.

So she followed.

Once inside, she took in the sparse surroundings as he set his hat on the rack near the door. She'd seen bachelor apartments with little furnishings before, but this was worse. There was a leather-looking recliner and a television wider than she was tall in the living room. A folding table with four folding chairs was near the kitchen.

"The first thing people ask is if I just moved in. Answer is no. I just don't need a lot of stuff. I only have the house for a tax break."

"Accumulating things takes time. You haven't even been here two years." He raised a questioning eyebrow and she realized her mistake. She shouldn't know that information.

"Speaking of where I live…how did you know? You drove straight here without my directions."

She fingered the closed blinds and peered between them to see if anyone was on the street. No one looked suspicious. A couple of men walked casually behind their self-propelled mowers on a Saturday afternoon, but no one else hung around.

"Oh, I keep tabs on people who owe me favors." That answer would have to do. But she needed to tell him how she really knew. Soon, but not now. She was still a little upset. "You aren't going to change the subject. I think you already know what I'm going to ask."

"Maybe. But why don't you ask anyway?" He brought one of the folding chairs from the kitchen and gestured for her to take the recliner. "We can go back and forth again like when you were sitting on my lap. That was fun."

Wade's tone was sort of casual, but she saw the curiosity in his eyes. She also didn't believe for a minute that it was the questions he found fun—maybe the sitting together. He was willing to share, but he wanted to know something. The look tempted her to spill everything before he could ask. But she had her own agenda and would have to take her chances.

"The world of gambling is more than familiar to you."

"That isn't a question, but the answer is yes. What I said at the track is true. Not a cover story."

His confession should have shocked her. But it fit him. Part of his charm was the way he talked people into situations. All three of the men he worked closely with had fallen for it. Shoot, she had fallen. It was why they were in this mess together.

"Like I said, I was raised by a gambler, a con man," he continued. "A bad one. A cheat. One who got caught. And caught often. Both by the law and the people he stole from."

Of all the things she'd imagined about him when she was younger or after he'd come back into her life again, the possibility of him being the son of a con artist had never ventured onto the radar. She had a thousand questions, but she sat silently and let him talk.

"When he wasn't picked up by the cops, we lived in cheap motels or crashed with one of his girlfriends. I wasn't much different. Not from him or the men who cheated him. That is, with the exception that when I got caught, I turned in my old man to stay out of jail. What does that make me?"

"Smart," she said without hesitation. "How did you get away?"

"From jail or the life?" He flipped the chair around and crossed his arms over the back. "An investigation that involved the state of Texas and a ranger who didn't give up. On anyone. Even me."

He looked relaxed now. Not ill like at the track, not anxious. Just comfortable.

"So that's why you applied to be a Texas Ranger?" It all made sense. "And that's how you got into law enforcement. Because the ranger who put your father in jail had your record sealed and raised you?"

He shook his head. "No." He sprang up and took down the only picture hanging on any wall.

"This is Fred and his wife, Faye." He tapped the people in the photo before handing it to her. "Somewhere they found money to send me to boarding school. It straightened me out. Changed that resentful fifteen-year-old kid to a man who wanted more. And yes, he wrote a letter of recommendation when I told him I wanted to make up for my misspent youth."

"That explains so much about you. Not this house, mind you." She looked around at all the space. "I still don't get why you don't have a couch."

"Are you going to tell me how you knew I lived here?" He'd sat backward on the chair again and tapped his fingers on his forearm, seemingly counting off the seconds until it was his turn to interrogate her.

"One more thing. Explain what happened at the track. Where's the money?" She'd almost been distracted enough to completely forget that she'd been upset regarding him taking over.

"Oh, yeah. Sorry I couldn't really explain everything when it was happening. But there was no way we could rig the race and actually collect that money."

"I wondered about that. So Dale Beauchamp works with you?"

"Yes. If Reval asks, we can say that we sort of cleaned the cash by placing the bet outside of the law's eyes. Sort of like structuring money or exchanging it for money orders, keeping the limits under ten grand. You know the routine."

"I'm halfway glad I don't. I'll trust you that the next time he asks for the money your associates will have it ready. But the last part... What makes you think they were trying to get us caught?"

"There would be an awful lot of questions if we placed a large bet—in cash—and then we won. So that had to be the real test. If we placed the bet and *didn't* get thrown in jail or at least detained, Reval would have known I'm undercover."

"Next time fill me in on the details. You took a risk that could have blown more than three years of my life."

"Promise." He stood, moved in front of her chair

and extended his hands. "This trust thing works both ways, you know."

She shamelessly placed her hands in his, letting him pull her to her feet. "Obviously I just proved that I trusted you by letting you take the lead at the track."

A good, solid answer. One that should deflect her earlier mistake about knowing where he lived. God, being in his arms sent shivers throughout her body. It was mind-blowing how primitively she reacted when he touched her.

He encircled her and tilted his head like he was about to kiss her, then raised it. This kiss might actually get them to the only real piece of furniture in the house...the bed.

Soft lips barely touched the sensitive skin where her neck met her shoulder. His teeth grazed her on the way to her earlobe. Then he stopped and so did the sizzle.

It was about to get real. Very real if he circled back to how she'd driven straight here without directions.

"Why do I have the feeling you know more about me than I do you?" he whispered. "Is Therese Ortis even your real name?"

Chapter Fourteen

Wade kept Therese close to him. He raised his head only long enough to ask his question. When she stiffened in his arms, he put his lips to work. Maybe the attempt to break through her resistance could be approached a different way. The direct questioning route sure wasn't working.

"My real name is Therese Maria Elisabeth Ortis. Born and raised in San Antonio." She stretched her neck back, giving him more access.

Wanting answers, but also wanting more of her bare skin against him, he continued his lips' quest across her shoulder.

"Is this going to be that back-and-forth thing you started? Am I supposed to admit something now?" He kept his words low and in between each nip along her skin.

"If you...want to," she said, sounding out of breath.

"You don't sound mad anymore."

"Concerned. I was..."

His fingertips found the edge of her shirt and

quickly shot underneath, taking in her smooth skin, pressing her breasts even closer to his chest.

"I think—" he planted his lips in the curve of her neck again "—that I—"

He raked the edge of his teeth up to her ear, following it with circles on her back.

Therese shivered against him.

Who the hell was he kidding? His actions weren't an interrogation—as if he ever thought they could be. He wanted her. She knew the truth about his history and still wanted him, too.

Dammit, he'd never felt like this. Open. Real. Excited about what came next. He drew back, staring at her beautiful face, waiting for her eyes to open and acknowledge the real him.

God, he'd turned into a sap. That was what nearly a year of desk duty and seeing his best friends find the women they love had done.

Therese opened her eyes. He waited for her to kiss him or at least expose her neck for him to take up his teasing again.

"Is this a good idea?" she asked instead.

"Getting to…um…know each other?" He slid his fingertips over the clasp of her bra. "Honestly, I think it's been a little one-sided."

Smiling, she drug a fingernail across his neck, then up and around the edge of his ear. His muscles tensed.

"You know that's not what I meant."

"I think you're assuming I can still think." He

lifted her off the floor, letting her body mold against him. "I am a man, you know."

Wade flexed his jaw along with other muscles as he tried to let Therese down. Her arms were around his shoulders, but she moved, resting more against him. She reached up to stroke his temple gently. He couldn't let her go.

"I think you're right about the talking. Let's chat with our bodies."

He was at a crossroads. The do-or-don't sign flashed on and off, on and off. One decision would keep him in a perpetual teasing state and the other led to sweet relief. But along with that relief came a commitment he'd never made or wanted before.

The pledge was right there, ready for him. The weight of Therese in his arms was less than the weight of that promise he wanted. Yeah, he wanted it all. Relief, connection, possible love.

Hell's bells, he had a beautiful woman in his arms and he was thinking about tomorrow. And the next day.

He shifted to keep her next to him, but with a little pop off the ground she lifted herself, wrapping her legs around him, and he kept her there. The movement hiked the small stretchy skirt she'd worn to the racetrack higher on her thighs. Closer to his face, she smiled before kissing him—winding her tongue around his.

Two seconds. That was all it took to make every bit of him rock-hard for her. It was like she'd read his thoughts and given her answer.

He was no longer questioning if he should or shouldn't. She'd made the decision when she settled her practically naked bottom against the skin of his forearm.

Wanting the bedroom, he stepped in its direction, but the lounge chair was closer. He got near and plopped his backside down, sinking into the leather. Therese stayed as close as possible until she shimmied onto her knees, placing them on either side of his thighs.

"Help me with this," she said, then laughed when she met his eyes.

He probably looked like a man who hadn't thought the chair all the way through. She continued to work at the zipper of her skirt, tugging, her arms behind her, thrusting her soft breasts closer to his face.

A man could only take so much cleavage that close before he had to...

Wade got out of the chair as fast as possible with Therese precariously balancing on his chest. Somehow in his rush, he scooped Therese into his arms instead of splaying her on the carpet. He bolted down the hallway, ready to drop her on the bed and devour every morsel of her delicious skin.

All of it. Every last inch of her.

"This is not good," he said stepping foot into the room.

With her arms around his neck, she burst out in a full-blown laugh. Her head dangled back, enticing him with more skin and sparkling eyes.

"I'm assuming there isn't a bed in the spare room with no clothes on top?"

Normally stacked inside his dresser, his clothes looked like they had all been upturned onto the unmade bed. *Jack*. "I don't keep it this way. Really."

"It doesn't matter."

"Jack or one of the other rangers grabbed stuff to leave at your place." He set Therese on her feet.

"It looks more like they took revenge on you for some reason." She spun around. "Unzip that, will you? I think there's a hook at the waistband."

He obliged and was mesmerized at how she gave the material a tug and it fell to her feet. She bent at the waist and picked it up, showing her heart-shaped derriere framed by a couple of strips of lace.

She folded her skirt and set it on the dresser next to his phone charging station. He watched her in the mirror as she crossed her arms and pulled off the matching top. Again he stared as she folded it and placed it with the skirt.

Wade took in her golden skin, the pale color of her lacy bra—even the tiny bows between her cleavage and on each side of her hips.

Therese cleared her throat, "The sooner we get this stuff put away, the sooner we can…get back to where we were. Unless you'd rather go back to the chair."

No chair. He shook his head.

But there was also no way he would wait until things were back where they belonged. No way.

He took giant steps to the end of the bed, pulled

the side of the blanket up and over the clothes and yanked until everything was on the floor.

"That's one way to take care of things."

He had his shirt over his head before she finished speaking. The belt followed while he toed off his boots. Yeah, everything landed on top of the mass of blanket and clothes. He didn't care.

The three triangles of lace beckoned. Teasing. Testing his limits of control. Ripping them off might be considered too...too something rude. His brain wasn't working, so it was probably true.

Man, did he want underneath those triangles.

Chapter Fifteen

Wade reached out, grabbing her hand as he jumped onto the bed, pulling Therese down with him. She giggled like a teenager. Maybe more like a nervous college girl. But she wasn't nervous.

Wade was just…fun. Their circumstances aside, she loved being with him.

He drew her next to him on top of the cool sheets. One arm under her head, the other under his own. She stared at the ceiling fan, spinning and cooling her skin.

Suddenly feeling awkward and not nearly as brave as when she'd disrobed, she tried to cover some of her midriff. But she wasn't going there. She would be bold and decisive with this man. She threw her arm out, landing on his chest.

Still watching the fan spin its blades in a circle, she drew the same shape across Wade's tanned chest, inching lower.

He drew in a deep breath through his teeth and captured her hand in his. "Whoa, how can you be so chilly?" He rubbed the back of her hand, keeping her fingertips just at the top of his jeans.

"Hey, not fair. There's still a major portion of you covered up." She gave a quick tug on a belt loop.

"Right." He popped up and tugged his jeans and socks off like they were on fire.

Maybe he was. She certainly needed the fan to cool off as he sat on the edge of the bed and slipped out of his boxers. The slight darkening of bruises from where he'd been hit by Rushdan's men almost brought her back to reality.

But instead she lay back on the bed on her elbows, watching him. Then he joined her, tangling their bodies together. She marveled at his warm, naked flesh touching every inch of hers.

The warmth soon became volcanic heat as he used all of himself—skin, hands and mouth—to touch most of her. Her cursed underwear was still between them.

"Did you answer your question?" he said before another round of strokes across her good lace bra.

"What?" she barely got out.

"About whether this is a good idea or not." He kissed his way to her belly button.

It is a super good idea. She enjoyed every second of his attention and wanted to be serious. But she laughed. Partly because his fingers slightly tickled and partly because he just made her feel good.

"Yes, my…my own question." *Oh, man.* How could she still think, let alone speak, with what he was accomplishing?

Wade kissed and explored and didn't ask any more questions. Her entire body shattered with reaction and kept her from thinking. Feeling became everything. The man used his hands—belly, hips, top of the lace, sides, bottom, then back to repeat. When his thumbs hooked the edges of the lace across her breasts, she clapped her hands over his to keep them still.

He paused until she slid her hands up his forearms. Then he gently raised her until his teeth could tease her nipples through the lace. Again and again he kissed, nipped and laved. Until…

"Enough!" she shouted, her voice bouncing off the ceiling and four walls. "Enough."

She pushed at Wade's shoulders, rolling him to his back. Sitting up, she bent her arms behind her back and unlatched the device she'd forever remember as being pure torture. She looked back at her partner, hoping she hadn't hurt his feelings.

Wade shamelessly grinned as her bra uncupped her breasts and fell to the bed.

"You did that deliberately." She quickly moved, shoving him deeper into the mattress, then sat across his lap and pinned him to the bed. Her intention had been to tickle him until he begged for mercy but that plan soon changed as they both realized where she was now located.

Wade's laughter became a raspy, long release of breath. His hands reached for her breasts but she leaned back, pushing their bodies closer together.

Then he sucked in a breath, holding it while she controlled their movements.

She allowed his thumbs to trace the remaining lace outline, closing her eyes before they gave away all the emotion she attempted to regulate. His breathing quickened as his hands skidded to her waist. She opened her eyes, seeing his closed as he spread his hands over her hips, pulling her down as his hips thrust upward.

She couldn't believe she was about to climax and technically they hadn't done… Well, technically. His jaw clenched as he kept them together but separate. Her hands slid across his chest, allowing her body to melt into his.

Then she exploded. An outburst that demanded all her energy and concentration. Wade used his body to keep her erupting. Weak with emotion, she collapsed onto his chest.

Wanting the same feeling for him, she pushed her panties aside, but he grabbed her hands, lacing his fingers through hers.

"Wait," he rasped. "We need…on the left."

How he kept his wits about him she'd never know. They needed protection. She rolled off him and scrambled to reach the nightstand. Wade didn't move. His breathing was still ragged or very controlled.

It was her turn to grin.

And drive him wild.

Already so close, she wondered just how long he'd last if she… She didn't need to think it through. Just do it.

She rolled the condom into place and stretched a leg across his, almost back where she'd enjoyed such tremendous pleasure. But she slid onto his thighs, teasing his belly with her fingers. Letting her long hair fall and caress until he swooped it into one hand and held one finger silently out to stop her.

"Therese," he pleaded in a whisper. "Forgive me."

Feeling and emotion rushed over her as Wade flipped her onto her back and they were one in an instant. But it wasn't over. Not for a while.

Wade had asked for forgiveness, but he didn't seem to be in a hurry. His body tensed and pulsed over her, around her, in her. She'd only thought she'd experienced pleasure minutes before.

Again and again he moved until they both reached a place she'd rarely been. They both stilled after one long appreciative kiss.

It was wonderful. Something she'd hold close to her soul for a very long time. She drifted off with the sweet thought of a lifetime of possibilities.

When she awoke, the room had gone from bright afternoon to a shadowy dusk. They'd slept for the past hour. She'd lay there watching the same fan turn in circles, attempting not to truly think about what she wanted. Or how much she hoped the assignment with Rushdan Reval would soon be over.

"Wade?" Therese gently shook his shoulder. "We should probably get up."

"Did you fall asleep?" he mumbled from his pillow.

"A bit. Too much on my mind."

Instead of getting up, Wade lifted her arm, rolled to his stomach and laid his head on her shoulder. He had a perfect view of her breasts, but his eyes had closed again. To his credit, the man was running on less than a couple of hours' sleep.

"My God, is today only Saturday?" she asked.

"Mmm," he sort of agreed. "You hungry?"

"Starving."

"I say we clean up and order some Italian. You like pasta? You aren't afraid of some carbs, are you?"

"I love carbs and I love Italian."

"Nice." He moved his free hand next to her head and played with her hair, bringing it across his face. "God, you smell good. Makes me hungry all over again."

"That's wonderful to hear. I thought I smelled like horses."

"Nope. Like peach ice cream."

"That's my shampoo. Peaches and cream."

His movements stopped and his breathing evened out as he fell back to sleep. Minutes passed and she gently freed her hair and tried to slide from under Wade.

"I'm awake," he said, lifting his head, but quickly dropped it again to her chest along with a quick kiss. "I'll see if Heath can pick up from Mariano's around the corner. He needs to take a look at the phone Sal gave us."

"I should probably get up, then." She tried once again to slide free from Wade's weight.

He moved quickly, placing a hand on either side of

her body and moving his over her completely. "You sure you're hungry?"

He lowered his mouth to hers, tangling their tongues as he tangled their legs. They kissed deeply, continuously as their bodies moved in an age-old rhythm again.

There was so much to talk about, so much to plan, to discover. But it could wait. She'd waited long enough for this human contact...however much he could give her, for however long.

Whatever happened between them, she could only hope it happened again and again.

Chapter Sixteen

Something had changed. Wade had a lump in his gut that had nothing to do with eating. The pasta he'd ordered for dinner had been fine. But somehow, something had changed.

He cared.

Before this afternoon, he had taken a beating to keep her safe. But now... The protectiveness that overwhelmed him could become a problem later on. Hell, he'd already gotten *the look* from Heath.

Heath had played the part of delivery boy. Italian food along with the necessary equipment to clone the burner phone Sal had given them. Not to mention his opinion about the unprecedented interagency cooperation he'd been observing.

But no one had any new information to clue them in on what Rushdan Reval, Public Exposure or another buyer would actually do with the algorithm. Everyone was still in the dark. By cloning the phone, the FBI, Homeland and the Texas Rangers could listen in and get up-to-the-minute knowledge about their movements and any instructions Reval sent.

The time frame Sal had originally set had long come and gone. The phone they'd been given sat between them on a TV tray. Every few minutes, Therese would pick it up, turn the screen on and then set it back down. No messages. No calls.

After Heath left, Wade tried to open his mouth a couple of times to ask what was wrong. Because things between them seemed awkward now. There were lots of reasons he should ask and one big one why he shouldn't. They were on the job. They couldn't afford to become any more distracted than they already were.

Right. No distractions.

Like watching her flip her hair off her shoulder or wanting to wrap the stray strand around his finger or use it to pull her to him for a kiss.

Therese was a helluva distraction. His mind was completely occupied by finding reasons not to take her back to bed. A great idea, but it had to wait until they no longer had to deal with Reval. Or find an algorithm before a domestic terrorist group bought it. An algorithm no one could speculate how dangerous it had become.

At least he hadn't thought about it. He hadn't had time. Since meeting up with Therese the day before, his sole focus had been making it through the next hour.

"What do you think this algorithm has morphed into?" he asked breaking the silence. "Six weeks ago it supposedly could take down an electrical grid."

"Chaos is the word most bandied about on the dark web."

"Chaos on what?"

"People paid a lot more than me only have theories. Most center around reasons terrorists would want a complicated algorithm. We interviewed all the members of Public Exposure without getting any closer. None of them knew specifics and their leader wasn't talking."

"Reval is just the go-between guy?" he asked.

She shook her head. "When he went to jail, I thought my undercover days were done. But I hung around Reval's organization tying up loose ends. Then you guys arrested the leader of Public Exposure six weeks ago. Word got out that the creator of the algorithm was looking for a new buyer. Reval wasn't involved before that."

"Then why is he now?"

"Since I was officially still a part of Reval's group they already had eyes on him. The FBI released him, hoping he could broker a deal. Homeland pushed the potential buyers in his direction by arresting others." She shrugged. "I haven't had any luck discovering details of the sale or exactly what the algorithm is capable of now that the programmer has upgraded it. Rushdan is keeping it very close to his fat chest."

"You think whatever reason he needs me will give you answers."

"Fingers crossed." She made the gesture with both hands. "The team has checked out all his known contacts. All dead ends."

"Does the computer guy who got my juvie records have something to do with it? How do we track him down?"

"We don't."

"What do you mean? It should be easy enough to find the info in Reval's office. Don't you have a warrant for his phone records? Together we should be able to find something written down."

"That's not our job." She gave a little shrug of acceptance—not anxious to explain.

"Wait a minute." He had to be misunderstanding. What the hell was their job if not to put Reval behind bars...for good.

"The team has checked out all his known contacts. All dead ends. Finding who has developed the algorithm is my objective. My primary goal. It won't matter if we stop whatever show they have planned for Dallas if we can't find the programmer."

"Show?"

"That's what they've called it recently. I've overheard Rushdan refer to it that way. The team is certain it's Rushdan's term for the terrorist attack."

"On Dallas? Do the rangers know about this? Local police?"

"I'm not certain. Prevention and cleanup aren't my jobs." She reached for the burner phone, checking it again.

"Wait...what?" He shook his head, unable to clearly comprehend what she'd just said. "What exactly is our job then? I thought we were taking down

Reval's organization and preventing the algorithm from being used."

"I tried to tell you this before, Wade. Sure, I want to put Rushdan Reval behind bars. But they may let his petty crimes go in exchange for the algorithm tech and developer."

"Petty? Rushdan's crime activities are no longer involved just locally. And attempting to kill me or others isn't what I'd call petty."

"You know what I mean. He's only a means for me to find the algorithm and the programmer. That's my objective. I have to find the person who created it. Hopefully before it's disbursed or sold."

The use of her singular "I" throughout her explanation didn't escape him. It stung like nothing he'd experienced before. She'd been in big trouble with Reval's men before she'd cozied up next to him at the bar.

Things like accomplishment credit usually rolled right off his back. Especially since he'd been sitting behind a desk while his fellow rangers had been stopping a serial killer, uncovering subversive FBI plots and keeping state analysts alive—a favor to this woman that had nearly gotten him killed.

Teamwork had resolved those cases and he'd been a part of getting the job done. Just like teamwork had gotten them farther along in this particular case. Or at least he'd thought it had. Dammit, were his feelings hurt? Or his ego?

Whatever it was, he had to let it go.

"I heard you say you were after the algorithm. I

kind of thought that's what I was helping with. One good break and we could grab Reval before he sells anything. Stop the terrorist group before they get started."

"That might not happen." Therese checked the phone, then moved to the window. "You need to get used to that idea."

"I get it. You've been at this a long time and it's hard to accept that you've needed help or that someone might have a different way of doing things."

She squinted in confusion. "*I* needed help? Hard for *me* to accept? Oh, really?" She crossed her arms and pressed her lips together into a straight line.

Damn.

"I just meant that working with me—with the Texas Rangers—might accelerate things a little. And plans might change."

"And you think I don't want to what? Share the credit? Stop acting like a bimbo? Stop having Rushdan or his men leer, touch and pinch me?"

"I didn't mean it like that."

"Oh, I see. Then you think I *like* being undercover. Or maybe I'm afraid to explain to my family exactly what's been going on so they might speak to me again? Or stop wondering if they'll be proud of me for what I've done over the past three years instead of thinking that I cheated on my police academy exam?"

"That's rough. I had no idea your family didn't know." His sympathetic thoughts slipped out. Then he witnessed a reaction that he was familiar with but hadn't seen. The feelings he'd had for so many of the early years with Fred rippled across Therese's face.

"I don't need you to feel sorry for me. This is a job."

"Right. Just a job." He hoped she meant the operation and not what had happened in the other room. For him the other room had been life changing and it was hard to focus on *just the job*.

She backed up and rested on the arm of his lounger but at least her arms weren't crossed in anger. "The FBI and Homeland are after the big fish, Wade. Some of the little ones will be thrown back."

"Meaning, they're already prepared to offer Reval a deal like the last time. Like the jail time he didn't serve for ordering his men to kill me."

"I don't have anything to do with the decision-making. Neither do you."

"Why not arrest him and make him cough up the programmer now? Why are we going through the motions?"

"We did that six weeks ago. The men who call the shots are prepared for the consequences."

"Even if innocent civilians get caught in whatever *show*—" he air-quoted the word to remind her what they were calling a terrorist plot "—Reval's customers are planning?"

"Can you drop this now? As a favor to me."

His hand flew to the pounding pulse in his temple, right above his injured eye. "Another favor? I'm not sure I can afford to. If you kept tabs on me like you said, you'd know how much your favors cost me."

Except no one knew about his loss of vision. Not even the doctors knew how much his peripheral was actually gone because he'd never been back to check. He was afraid they'd bench him. So he'd kept the loss to himself.

"I'm very aware of what happened. And I know how frustrating it must be to hear this. But you have to try to see the big picture. The algorithm is more important than you or me."

"I don't get it, Therese. Why can't the aim be to get both?"

The phone rang as Therese shook her head.

"Preventing a national emergency doesn't take into consideration our personal preferences. I just wanted to warn you that Rushdan Reval might make a deal."

Wade watched Therese click the speaker button knowing they hadn't left their debate in a good place.

"He wants you at his club. Now," Sal's voice boomed through the little cell.

"Wade's proven he knows what he's doing, Sal. Give the phone to Rushdan." Therese had shifted to that bimbo-like tone, coaxing men to comply. "Come on, Rushy, I know you're listening."

"Get here within the hour, Therese," the greedy, double-chinned slob answered. "I have a job for you. Leave the phone with your new boyfriend. We're moving forward."

"But we don't have the money yet. Don't you need me to bring that to you?" Therese asked.

"The money doesn't matter. It never mattered

other than I like to have an abundance. I had to make sure Ranger Wade was sincere and didn't hold any grudge for the boys trying to dispose of him last year."

"Then I'll keep it." Wade threw in to let the man know he'd been listening. "That will just about get the guys I owe off my back."

"Probably. But you still need to earn it." Reval made a disgusting sound, like slurping through his teeth.

"No more tests, please. It's too risky, Rushy. Can't you just tell us what you need?" Therese coaxed.

Listening, someone might get the impression she actually believed those words. But watching her, Wade could see that her body language showed she hated saying them. She was good. Really good at what she did. But what was she up to?

"We ran to the track for you. Then we've been sitting here so long just waiting. There's only so much golf a girl can watch. I got things to do, Rush baby. You don't pay me to be a babysitter," Therese complained.

"Funny you should mention that, Therese. I have another chore for you. Sal will pick you up at the club."

"Is an hour soon enough? I need to swing by my place and change."

Wade stood, searching for a reason he should be going with Therese. They should stay together. Right? Didn't she realize that?

"That'll be fine. And Ranger Wade?" Reval said.

"Yeah?"

"Don't bother following Therese. When I send your instructions they'll be timed from your house. And yes, I know where you live." The phone disconnected.

"What the hell was that?" Wade demanded.

"My job."

"I thought your job was to find the algorithm."

"My job is to do anything Rushdan Reval tells me to do so we'll find the algorithm and programmer."

"You can't go. Not like this." He put his hands out, but she grabbed her purse instead.

"When I'm summoned, I go. That's my role in all this."

"I can call him back, demand that you stay with me. We're a team."

She arched a perfectly shaped eyebrow and pulled her keys from her small purse before hanging the strap across her shoulder. "If there's one thing I've learned being undercover, it's that you're out here on your own. You should get used to it."

She was out the door the next instant. What if that was the last time he saw her? What if she did her disappearing act again? What if Reval…? He yanked the door hard enough to bounce off the wall as he pounced onto the porch.

"Wait!"

By the surprised look on Therese's face, she hadn't thought he'd follow her. But he had—still unsure how to handle their differences and damn sure he didn't want this woman to disappear from his life.

"I took an oath to protect the people of Texas. And I don't take my promises lightly. It's hard for me to let harm come to anyone if I can prevent it. Stop the threat, then find the next. I don't think I can do what you're asking me."

"Don't worry about it, Wade. We aren't really a team but it was fun pretending while it lasted. I'll handle this my way. I can take care of myself." She continued to her car. "Don't forget to watch your back, hon. Since I won't be there to do it."

Smiling at him over the top of the sedan, she opened the door and slid behind the wheel like everything was perfect. Wade watched, completely dumbfounded. Sometime in the last fifteen minutes his heart had been ripped from his chest. There was a big gaping hole making him wonder if it could ever be the same.

Why didn't any of this seem to bother her as much as it bothered him?

Chapter Seventeen

Therese's hands shook so hard she couldn't fit the key in the ignition. She wanted to stay put in her apartment. For the first time, she was actually afraid to face Rushdan. Walking out Wade's door was the second hardest thing she'd ever done. Facing her siblings, aunts, uncles and other family after leaving the San Antonio police academy in disgrace had been the worst.

"I hate this," she shouted as she pounded the steering wheel.

Deciding to be a police officer had cost her all of her friends from high school and college. Being a hot shot at the academy hadn't gotten her any new ones. So leaving them behind for an undercover job had been easy at first. Until the lies became everything her life was based on.

After a while it gets hard to remember there was a different reality.

No one knew the truth except her handler, and that person had changed with each year. Currently it was Steve Woods and Megan who had been in her academy class. None of them really knew the person she'd been before this.

And now Wade. She'd wanted to be truthful with him for a long time. Now he knew. So why did it still feel like she was lying?

What had she expected? Gratitude for all her sacrifice? Maybe empathy or even a big "wow." Any of those would have been better than the stunned silence and pity she'd read on his face.

Dropping her head onto her arms, she wanted to cry. But there wasn't time. She needed to get to Rushdan's club instead of Sal taking her to the office. And only had half an hour to do it.

The end game was in sight and she'd soon be able to put all her own self-pity to rest. She drove quickly to the seedier side of Deep Ellum, close to Second Avenue. The Reveille wasn't the darkest, dankest dive around…but it was close.

Pulling into the gravel parking lot, she noticed several of the street lights were out again. It happened all the time. No big deal, but when she caught the kids throwing rocks at them, they normally received a hefty piece of her mind. That wouldn't be high on her priorities for long.

She glanced at her wrist. Among the many hoop bracelets she'd added to her outfit tonight was a watch. She was on time. Before she patted herself on the back, she noticed movement in the shadows to her left. She had to stay in character, had to ignore Sal and pretend to be oblivious.

Therese forced herself to shrink back when he

finally showed himself. Good grief, she wanted to stand nose-to-nose with Rushdan's go-to man and take him down. Drawing on the desperateness she'd felt earlier, she pushed it to the top of her frayed nerves, faking a little scream.

"Oh my God, Sal. You scared the living daylights out of me."

Whatever Sal was doing, his real intention was to intimidate her, and she had to let him. At least a little. That was her part in all this mess. The end was near. She clung desperately to that.

She looked around for Wade's truck. She hated to confess that she had hoped it would be there. Even as much as she hated involving him the night before, she wanted him there by her side.

Upset, confused. A little scared for what was coming. It all mixed together inside her head, making it hard to think straight. Right. That was it. She didn't need Wade to protect her. But that wasn't the point. It wasn't her need. It was her want, her desire. She wanted Wade nearby and wanted to work with him.

"The boss is waiting inside. You know he don't like to wait." Sal puffed on a cigarette, then tossed it to the ground.

"I got here as quickly as I could. Put that silly thing away." She gestured to the 9mm he had pointed at her. "It might actually go off and hurt someone."

Carefully maneuvering the gravel in three-inch heels, she clicked the alarm on her car and headed to the club. She'd been treating Sal like that since she'd been promoted in Rushdan's organization two years ago.

Blunt force dead center in her back sent her tumbling to her knees. There was no way to stop it. Once on the ground, a booted foot across her shoulder blades kept her there.

Her face had landed on the solid slab of concrete at the club's back entrance instead of the gravel that bit into her flesh. She could feel the sting of scrapes on her knees and the palms of her hands.

Sal pressed his boot into her flesh. The barrel of his handgun pinched the base of her neck.

"You listen real close, bitch. I know something ain't right. You might have the boss wrapped around your finger but you're gonna give me more respect. If ya don't…" He twisted the barrel, tangling the long strands of hair behind her ear. "I'll be explainin' to the boss man how you met with an accident."

"Respect. Got it. May I get up now?"

The vibration through her body thrummed so loud in her ears she was certain Sal could hear it. She'd just thought her hands had been shaking with anger before. Maybe it was good that they physically moved as Sal helped her to her feet. It certainly let him know that he'd scared her.

The heels wobbled under her unsteady legs, forcing her to grab Sal's forearm. She hated to, but it was either that or fall to the gravel a second time. He laughed.

Please let it be me that slaps the cuffs on this waste of skin.

The jerk didn't open the door for her. She hadn't really expected him to, but this time she wrapped her hand around the doorknob and found it locked. Her stomach rolled with uncertainty. She nearly lost it as she bent over to pick up her keys. Sal's smackdown had her spooked.

"What will Rushdan say about this?" she asked, forcing her voice to remain steady and ooze confidence.

Lies and more lies. The barrel against her skin had her more shaken than she liked to admit.

Pull yourself together.

"Go ahead and ask him."

Oh my God. It was last night all over again. And this time, she couldn't run to Wade to save her. She had to face Rushdan and hope there was a reason he wouldn't listen to Sal and allow him to kill her.

Still with a gun pointed at her back, she rounded the corner and saw Rushdan holding court with the young women who served drinks. It was early enough in the evening that the bar wouldn't have very many customers, but she searched the room. The official manager was nowhere in sight.

No other staff. Just the girls. Another glance at the front door and she noticed the bolt.

Sal crossed his arms—gun still in his hand—and planted himself between her and the back exit. No one would get out of the bar unless Rushdan allowed it.

The other women probably didn't realize they were hostages. They were chatting away, fawning over the bar owner, vying for attention or his notice. Hoping they might be the next girl Rushdan brought up the ranks. Someone to be her replacement?

Oh, God. She'd played right into their hands. It wasn't an accident that she'd overheard Rushdan's phone conversation that he needed someone in law enforcement to make sure the show happened. Then the threat had come from the two last night and she'd sailed directly into Wade's arms.

He knew.

She'd been set up. Been used like the pawn she was supposed to be. As much as she hated Rushdan Reval, the man was smart. Now he'd separated them.

Whatever Rushdan needed Wade to do, it was about to happen and she wouldn't be there to make certain it did. Wouldn't be there to make certain Wade chose finding the program and programmer over saving the day. Joining him to follow through on her mission... By the look on Rushdan's face, that wasn't going to happen.

"Sit down, Therese. Join me in a drink."

"What's going on, Rushy?" Her heart raced along with her mind.

"You'll learn soon enough. Get my special phone, Sal." He snapped his fingers like he was summoning a waiter.

The snap brought Therese to focus. Everything she'd been thinking vanished with the look on Rushdan's face. Fury filled his eyes. What had happened?

The right-hand man left through the front door

and a new minion Therese didn't know took his place at the back of the room.

"I thought you needed me for something special."

He stared at her skinned palms she'd placed on top of the table and then he smiled. She slowly drew her hands into her lap to keep his thoughts on the now instead of the previous night. But the two accomplices he'd sent to kill her or chase her into Wade's protection were at the front door.

"You don't think a night out with me is something special, my dear?"

"Of course. But if we're taking over one of your bars for the night, it feels kind of weird to keep all the waitresses around. I can get you whatever you need since I know where it is."

"They're staying." His voice turned dark with an angry vibration. It was one of the rare times she'd seen the horrible man Rushdan Reval actually was erupt to the surface.

"Are they... Rushy, they kind of look like...like hostages."

No. She couldn't let all these women be hurt because of his suspicions.

"They won't be as long as your boyfriend follows through. Right now they're my alibi."

"I could take care of that. You don't really need them."

"Don't test my patience, Therese. Keep everyone in line and you'll all be fine."

The menacing look in his eyes as he'd chimed that they weren't hostages shouted that they actually were. She'd been the only one to see it or it would have scared all the women. It verified one thing she'd known all along. Rushdan wasn't afraid to get rid of them all. Especially if Wade failed.

What if the Texas Ranger followed his conscience or his desire for revenge? What if he told the rangers about whatever Rushdan had planned? There were five souls depending on him and he didn't even know it.

She regretted not talking things through with Wade before she'd left. Her self-righteousness might have just gotten them all killed.

Chapter Eighteen

*Go to the private entrance at Love Field Airport.
You'll be met with instructions.*

Great. Would it be Therese meeting him? Maybe
Sal.

Wade drove past the entrance, searching from his
truck for a possible ambush—nothing in sight, no
one around. The entrance looked normal and deserted for a Saturday night. Deserted might be normal. He didn't know.

He parked across the street, keeping his eyes open
for his backup. He could only assume all the agen-
cies involved in this operation had listened in on the
phone call that gave him the instructions. Major Clements wouldn't send him inside without backup. He
just had to trust it would be there when he needed it.

Two men lurked at the edge of the building shadows. He lifted his hands slightly in the air, waiting
on them to indicate which way he needed to go. One
man he recognized from Reval's office building. The
big guy who'd hit him a couple of times. The other
wore glasses and cradled a laptop in his arms.

Was luck on his side today? Could this be the elusive programmer Therese was so hot to catch? He caught himself cracking a smile and stopped.

"You guys going to tell me what's going on?"

"Should we check him for a wire?" the big guy asked the nerd.

"We don't have time." He began walking to the gate. "Come on. Come on."

"To do what? I haven't been instructed—"

"You just need to get us inside. Then escort us to one of the planes owned by your group," the nerdy guy squeaked.

"Now hold on. You mean a DPS plane? I wouldn't know where the Department of Public Safety keeps part of its fleet. This is a little outside my comfort zone." He needed more information.

"Don't worry, just get us inside."

"Easy for you to say. I need to talk with your boss."

"Mr. Reval isn't available. Just do what you do and get us inside the airport." Rushdan's man pulled up the edge of his shirt, showing the handle of a handgun.

"Is that supposed to intimidate me?" Wade pushed his fingers through his hair, then smoothed it back down. "To get inside, I'll be forced to sign in. That means this is a one-time deal. I think your boss might want to know that."

"Everything's been planned, Hamilton. Just get us through those gates and past the guards," the little nerd demanded.

Wade shrugged. He still didn't have a clue about what would happen. If he had to take down these two, he could. Therese might be angry… Who was he kidding, she'd be furious and that would probably be the end to a relationship that had barely got off the ground. But he couldn't allow these clowns to launch an attack on Dallas.

Right?

With no concrete evidence, he had to play it by ear. Waiting to decide was a logical choice, not just an excuse to try to let it unfold Therese's way. Then why did he feel guilty that he'd be stealing all of Therese's glory?

They approached the gate and Wade took out his badge. The security guard turned out to be an excited kid.

"Evenin'," Wade said, holding his ID up and purposely keeping his fingers over his name. "Mind if we visit our hangar?" Hell, he didn't know if the Rangers had a hangar or not.

The kid pulled out a clipboard. "Not at all. I just need your names." He looked up, pen in hand, ready to write.

"That's the thing. It would be better if we didn't leave the reporters anything to report."

"But I might get into a lot of trouble."

Wade dropped a hand on the kid's shoulder. "I promise after this case breaks open to come back and update your log or talk with your supervisor. I'll be sure to let him know how helpful you were."

"Aw, man, that would be really nice of you. The

hangar's a long way. Do you want to borrow the golf cart?"

"You're all right kid. Thanks," the big guy answered.

"No problem. Here's the key." He took a lanyard from around his neck and held it out.

The big guy snatched it with his thick hands while Wade put his ID away. His two companions got on the front bench, leaving him to sit backward. The big guy took off, pedal to the floor.

"Slow down, Nico. Don't draw attention to us," the nerdy guy insisted.

"That was too easy." What kind of a guard just handed everything over—even young inexperienced ones? "Yeah, way too easy," Wade muttered.

"Just go with the flow, Hamilton." Nico turned to look at him and forgot to steer, sending the cart—and them—swaying back and forth.

Bracing himself between the bars, Wade twisted around to look at the guard's booth. Sure enough, the kid was on the phone, pointing in their direction. *Good for you, kid.* But no luck for him tonight.

"We need to ditch this cart." He could see flashing lights from the opposite end of the airfield. "Ditch it now!"

Nico slammed the cart to a halt, drawing his weapon when his feet hit the ground.

"Put that thing away and get to the side of that hangar."

They ran to the metal hangar wall, Nico pounding into it and making enough noise to wake the dead—

or alert Love Field police—whichever happened first. The nerd panted like he'd run a marathon.

"Take care of those cops," he huffed and puffed through his words, "while we do what we came to do."

Wade couldn't let these guys out of his sight. No way. He had to know what they were implementing with that laptop.

"No." He turned and used both hands to grab the nerd by his shirt collar. "Tell me what you need."

"I can't."

"You should have from the get-go and we wouldn't be in this mess. Now what do you need? What are you trying to do?"

The lights were getting closer. The little man's eyes darted back and forth under his glasses. Nico— the big guy who Wade owed a punch to the gut— tugged at Wade's hands.

"All right. I need to test some software."

"Give it to me. I can get in and out without the two of you slowing me down."

"I... I can't."

"It's either that or we all go to jail. You and Reval should have been upfront about this and I would have come up with a plan. A much better plan." He released the man's collar and backed up. "I should hand you over to the cops and maybe I can talk my way out of this mess."

Nico chambered a round. He made a huge mistake by acting all tough guy and keeping it by Wade's ear. Wade whipped his elbow into Nico's gut, then as Reval's gunman doubled over, Wade shoved a fist into the thug's nose.

Nico dropped his weapon, grabbing his face and moaning.

"Sorry about that, tough guy, but I owed you one." Wade quickly knelt and hid the gun in his boot. "Instructions. Fast. Then get lost. If you're caught by the cops, it's trespassing and Reval can bail you out."

"You can't do this," the nerdy guy said as Wade pulled the laptop from his fingers. "You need my expertise."

"Watch me. Now what do you need?"

With blood smeared across the side of his face, Nico had a recognizable look in his eyes—revenge. But he reached into his pocket and pulled out a folded piece of paper. Nerdy guy watched him, shaking his head from side to side, mumbling something about Wade being not only a cop but a stupid one.

Wade crumpled the paper into his palm and ran. He made it to the corner of the building before looking around. The police cars split in two directions. The men he'd walked through the gate with were nowhere in sight.

Squinting at the paper in the dark shadow of the building, he could see that it was a list for the morons he'd parted ways with. Beginning with meeting him at the west airport gate.

Nerdy guy didn't seem to be the programmer. Wade wasn't lucky—unless he didn't get caught by the police currently circling around every building.

He squatted at the corner and held the note in the edge of the light, barely making out Building Six.

Feeling like he was in a World War II POW movie, he avoided searchlights and the airport police. He finally made it to Building Six and parked himself between the recycling cans and some decorative bushes.

There was no way he had the algorithm on this laptop. The directions said nothing about any kind of attack or uploading any type of file. Waiting for the police searchlights to fade in the distance, he walked up to an unlocked door and went inside the dark office.

"Stay right where you are."

"Don't move."

"Freeze!" Laughter. "You know I've always wanted to say that."

Greeted by three familiar voices…music to his ears. Maybe his luck was holding after all.

Chapter Nineteen

Therese sat at the corner table with the other four women. Regulars came to the door, found it locked and would tap on the window close to her. She could only shrug and smile. She pretended to be just as clueless as to what was going on.

Rushdan had practically admitted that this was his alibi for whatever task he'd sent Wade to complete. So here she sat while he flipped the "special" phone Sal had brought to him. He hadn't used it yet.

It looked like any other cell phone as he dropped it inside his jacket pocket. In fact it was identical to the one he took from another pocket. The special phone could be what he used to contact the programmer. She needed that phone.

"God, I'm hungry. Do you think we could order a pizza, Therese?" Julie Anne asked.

"I'd go in on that," Rachel said.

Therese got up and wove through the empty tables to her boss. "Any chance we could order or have one of the guys pick us up a pizza from around the corner?"

With his back to her, she hadn't noticed he was on the phone.

Rushdan turned on a dime and Therese couldn't avoid the backhand that came along with it. She didn't fake the painful moan that escaped before she had control. The staggering blow was meant to hurt and intimidate. He raised his hand to hit her again but she blocked it.

"I'm not telling you what I want done. If the cops get their grubby paws on that laptop, I'll kill you myself." Rushdan's eyes were huge in his red, puffy face. He looked like he'd pop with the prick of a pin.

If only she had a pin.

Too late she realized that her arm still blocked his second blow. She wasn't supposed to be quick or competent enough to accomplish that. Still rubbing her face where his hand had connected, she tried to drop her arm to her side. It was caught by one of the men she didn't recognize.

"Why are you bothering me, Therese? What did you hope to gain besides irritating me?" Rushdan finally asked before putting his concentration back into his phone.

Therese yanked her arm free. "The girls need a restroom break. And if we're just sitting there, is it okay to order a pizza?"

"I don't have time for this! Your stupid boyfriend can't complete one task I give him. First the money and now this! I expected something. But this is out-rageous. Get him on the phone. Now. Immediately."

Rushdan paced the length of the bar. Therese had

never seen him frantic, ranting as he tossed his regular phone to one of the guys to dial. His plans must have gone wrong.

Her mind had been working on a way she could keep her cover if Wade stormed the bar and arrested everyone. He must have somehow stopped the attack. Why would Rushdan look so confused if everything had gone well?

Wade was willing to blow everything—including her cover—to bring down Rushdan. She had to be ready.

"Is there anything I can do to help?" she asked timidly while taking steps away from Rushdan.

"Get me a good shot of whiskey. The stuff that's behind the bar is terrible." It might be watered down, but Rushdan still finished what was in his tumbler.

"I'll need to go in the back for the good stuff."

Rushdan tossed his chin up, essentially giving her permission to walk around Sal. Therese tried to remain confident as she passed him in the narrow hallway that held the restrooms. But Sal stayed where he was as she entered the storeroom and secured the boss man's whiskey.

Wait. If Rushdan knew she and Wade were undercover—wasn't that the reason he was treating her this way? Then why would he be confused if Wade hadn't completed his assignment? Good grief. Wade hadn't thrown her assignment away... he'd completed it. That had to be the reason Rushdan was confused.

Wade had followed through.

She felt the outline of her phone in her trouser pocket and was tempted to call Wade. Tempted, but something didn't feel right. Rushdan was out in the open, something he never did.

She abandoned the idea of phoning Wade, deciding to wait it out. Whatever was going on, her instincts told her it wasn't the big "show." So she'd concentrate on getting the girls pizza and keeping them safe. Keeping her fingers crossed that Wade hadn't taken the easy arrest and would wait to get his revenge.

Bottle in hand, she reached behind the bar on her way past and grabbed a clean tumbler.

Rushdan was on the phone, looking into it like a video call. "Bring the laptop back to me, Hamilton, or I'm afraid Therese will…"

Rushdan pointed the phone at her. Sal stepped in front of Therese and threw a right punch into her stomach. The tumbler rolled free from her hand on one side as the whiskey bottle shattered on the other when she hit the floor.

"You son of a bitch, leave her alone!"

Wade? Not here. Just the phone. He was on the phone.

No acting necessary. She hadn't seen the punch coming and sent a major shock through her body. Julie Anne rushed to her side, helping her into a chair. It took several seconds before she could breathe regularly again or talk.

It wasn't the first time she'd been hit. And from the reactions of the other women, they'd all seen something like it before. It was her fault they were all here. So she was glad to see them retreat farther into the corner. They looked a little more relaxed knowing it was Therese who would take the beating.

Now she knew why they were there...to keep her in line. She may be a hostage he would threaten to kill. But she was the leverage to ensure Wade behaved correctly.

Covered in whiskey, she turned to Julie Anne, "Snag me a couple of clean towels from behind that post, please."

Julie Anne did it in as small a way as possible. Therese didn't blame her. Sal stood close by, ready to attack. Once the towels were in her hands, she waved the young woman back to sit with the others. Dabbing up the whiskey around her face and neck, she hid her eyes and took in where all the men were.

Rushdan pushed a drink into her hands. "This will help, my dear."

She tried to fake some calm. She couldn't, but who would? So she acted naturally and swallowed the cheaper whiskey he'd poured in one long gulp. Then she looked into the face of evil... Rushdan.

"I should have killed that tin star bastard when he showed back up last night. What made me think I could use him?" He paced a few seconds then looked directly at her. "Or you."

Rushdan marched to her and backhanded her again. Her head snapped from right to left but this time she concentrated, keeping her breathing even. At least both cheeks would be equally red and swollen.

"Put her in the car," Rushdan ordered, pulling a stack of cash from his money clip. "I'm sure the rest of you could use a couple of hundred in tips tonight to keep quiet."

At least the women would be okay. Sal tried to jerk her up from the chair. She didn't move. She took deep breaths, controlling the urge to rub the sting away. But it was more than just defiance. She needed to hear everything Rushdan said.

She couldn't do that from the car.

Had Wade called Rushdan or had it been the other way around? She forced herself to think. Right. Rushdan had been screaming for someone to get Wade on the phone. What had happened in those precious minutes she'd been thinking in the storeroom? "I said put her in the car." Rushdan seemed to have control of his voice again.

Sal shrugged as she jerked her elbow from his grasp.

"I can walk all by myself. I've been doing it for years. Even in heels." She stood, catching her hip on the nearby table, but keeping the "ouch" all to herself.

Sal walked closely behind her. She could see him in the bar mirror. Rushdan finished paying the women and hurried them out the front door. None of them picked up their purses from the top of the bar.

Therese raised a finger, trying to catch them, but couldn't say anything. It was hard just putting one foot in front of the other. Each upright step was a major accomplishment. Okay, maybe she was a bit more loopy from the gut punch or that shot of whiskey than she originally thought.

Before she made it to the hallway, Rushdan latched on to her elbow, pulling her to a stop. Her heels were slick on the floor as he spun her around.

"Feeling a bit tipsy, Therese?" he laughed.

She tried to nod, but her vision went a little wonky with a lot of blinking, before the world turned completely black. Wade wouldn't be storming the place coming to her rescue.

But the night was young.

"CAN'T YOU GO any faster?" Wade asked, knowing it was the fifth or sixth time since he'd seen Therese get punched.

"Creating a fake that looks as good as the real thing isn't as easy as I make it seem." The FBI computer specialist returned to clicking away at his keyboard on the other side of the office.

Jack dropped a hand on Wade's shoulder. "I know this is tough, but he's doing the best he can."

"He said I had an hour. I need over half that long to get to that address."

"Reval isn't going to hurt her." Jack grimaced. They all knew she'd been hurt with that punch.

"You're right." Wade continued to stare at his phone, watching the estimated arrival time change on his map app. "He's got guys to do it for him."

"Thinking like that is going to get in your way," Heath said, leaning back in a desk chair in the corner. "I can tell you that from recent experience."

"I think we all can," Slate added.

Wade put the phone in his back pocket. Reval wouldn't call him again. He probably wouldn't hurt Therese. Or have Sal touch her. At least not until Wade arrived with the damn laptop.

Then he might kill them both.

Heath was right. Thinking like this was messing with his mind, his training and any plans that needed to be made to ensure he and Therese weren't killed.

"Look, guys. I appreciate that you're here supporting me. But is it necessary for *all* of you to hang around?"

"You're just lucky Major Clements was required to hang back at the task force headquarters. Talk about impatience. He'd be wondering why all of this wasn't done in advance." They all laughed at Jack's observation.

"I got to ask you guys." Wade looked at his three best friends in the world. "What would you have done if those other two clowns had shown up?"

"Arrested them," they said in unison.

His friends and partners all nodded their heads and stopped talking. Arms crossed, each leaning on something, all more worried than they were letting on. He didn't want to be dramatic, but none of the cases any of them had worked on were as important as this. He wouldn't say it aloud, but they all knew it.

The "show," as potential buyers on the dark web had been referring to it, had the potential to be another 9/11. Therese hadn't been exaggerating. She'd been right about its importance, but wrong that she wasn't a part of the team. There was a huge team of people working on this.

This team. His team.

That was why these men were all here for him. Waiting with him. Keeping him sane.

"Maybe you should go over what the task force has come up with one more time," Heath said, breaking the silence.

"I got it," Wade told him.

"It can't hurt. Remember, Heath couldn't recall which one of us he'd sent to find his daughter," Slate reminded them.

"It can't hurt." Jack slapped Wade's back again. "When the specialist over there is finished, you'll have a fake schedule for the private airplanes arriving at Love Field and the surrounding smaller airports. Reval just clued us in on his buyers and their arrival times."

"I don't get why he needed this. Wouldn't they all contact him?" Wade had listened and accepted the information and reasoning handed to him earlier. But the guys were right, hearing it and then processing it were different. This time around, parts just didn't add up.

"It might be that he doesn't have specific information," Jack told him. "Or maybe he's worried competition might be headed this way, too. Maybe you'll get him to fess up why he needed it."

"Aren't we tipping our hand if he does and knows this one is a fake?"

"Possibly," Jack agreed. "If that happens, we'll ride in to save you and your princess."

"I wouldn't let Therese hear you refer to her as a princess or even a lady in distress," Slate joked, bending his arm to show off his muscles. "Have you seen the guns on that woman's arms? I'm sure she's okay, man."

Heath got that what-if look on his face and raised a finger. "I'm going to have the computer specialist check something. Be right back."

That look—or thought process—had saved them on more than one occasion. If it saved his hide tonight, it would be saving Therese, too.

"What are the three of you going to be doing while I'm risking my neck?"

"Getting the job done," Slate told him with a straight face.

"Don't worry about our end—or the task force—we've got your back. Just like you've had ours," Jack told him.

The words meant more than he'd thought. *Damn.* Therese had never had that. She'd been completely isolated for the past three years. No friends, family or coworkers. It made it easier to accept that she'd walked away from him so quickly that afternoon.

Or at least he'd thought it had been easy for her. Maybe not.

The guys—his fellow Texas Rangers—had him covered. They'd penned him to the wall to keep him in that office after Therese had been hit by Sal.

Maybe that was why two of them were still between him and the exit.

Needing to focus, he brought his phone back to his hand to stare at it once again. Focus evaded him except for one thought. Reval.

He'd been determined to bring Reval down before. There wouldn't be any deals for the common scum. He'd be in front of every judge and prosecutor to make certain that didn't happen.

A year ago he'd felt anger at nearly being blown up. Anger at how stupid he'd been to go at it alone and let Reval's men get the jump on him. But he'd gotten over it. Or at least he thought he had, until he'd found out Reval was out of jail.

The past six weeks hadn't just been about searching for Therese. In the back of his mind, he knew she wouldn't be far from Reval. Someday he'd let her know just how right she'd been to question what his true motivation was today.

Reval was going down. Away. For good. Without parole or deals.

But not before Wade got a piece of him. And not before Wade severely chastised Sal for hitting his girl.

Chapter Twenty

Therese awoke in the dark with a headache the size of Dallas. She was on a couch in Rushdan's office, blinds drawn. Alone. Where would he keep important, secret information? She let her eyes search for obvious cameras. None. Envisioned the sleek glass desk. Limited drawer storage only in the bookcase.

There had to be a safe in the wall, the floor, behind the books. That meant they needed a combination. Three years and she still didn't know. But what was most likely his special phone—as he'd called it—would still be in his pocket.

Swinging her feet to the floor, she slowly pushed herself up and staggered to the private bathroom. Even after shutting and locking the door, she could hear the fish tank gurgling as she examined her split lip and slightly discolored cheeks.

"You look absolutely terrible," she told her reflection.

She quickly washed the blood from her face and pulled her fingers through her hair. The bathroom had as little decor as Rushdan's office. No pictures with glass that she could break. No heavy statues to swing. Just the bare necessities.

"The Bare Necessities."

She returned to the couch, humming the Disney song that had popped into her head. She didn't walk the room physically. It was too dangerous and she didn't know if she could. She should let Rushdan return and see her acting obedient.

God, she felt loopy. Light. No, it was more of a heavy feeling like she couldn't get up. Weird. Or drugged.

That was why she'd passed out so fast.

So she continued to hum and look around the room for any indication of a safe. It had to be here. Rushdan didn't have any other offices. She kept staring at the walls, but her headache distracted her.

The song earworm took her back home to San Antonio. She couldn't shake it out of her mind. She was certain there was something else she should be doing. Being the oldest, she'd been the resident babysitter when her parents took extra shifts or the rare times they went out. Her siblings had watched a ton of sing-along movies. The words drifted through her mind, urging her to close her eyes.

But instead of cartoons or animated images, she was suddenly in the passenger seat of a car. Eighteen. Stuck in her boyfriend's wrecked Camaro. The darkness surrounded her. No dashboard or streetlights. They'd been out in the country on a little known state highway when a deer ran across the road. They'd crashed.

Wade.

She hadn't known him. She didn't know his name until she'd read it in the paper. He wasn't a Texas Ranger at the time, just a Texas Department of Safety highway patrolman. It was the only time in her life she'd been rescued and she'd never forgotten his face. A couple of years later she'd seen it again with his promotion to the Company B Rangers and she'd been following his career ever since.

If it hadn't been for the hero crush she'd had on Wade she would never have joined the police academy or been recruited for this undercover position. So, in a way, all of this was Wade's fault. The bloody lip, the headache, the undercover life-threatening moment... *Yep, all of it.*

She laughed hysterically. Out of control, she couldn't stop.

"Therese, my dear. Wake up."

She opened her eyes from the strange, disturbed sleep. Rushdan had his hand on her shoulder. Sal had his hand on his gun.

"Are you okay, my darling?"

Now she was his darling? Hardly.

"I'm fine. Just a bad dream." She scooted across the white leather sofa, away from Rushdan.

Too late she remembered the phone. Back in his jacket pocket? Back in a safe? They needed that special phone. Before she could return to his side, he stood and went to his desk.

"You've been out for a long time, Therese. I had no idea you were so...delicate." He massaged the back of his hands, then dismissively waved at Sal. "Leave us."

She waited for the door to shut before saying, "You love doing that."

"Yes. I love being in charge and making everyone else scurry around trying to stay on my good side."

"Being the big, important man," she mumbled.

"Don't be afraid to speak up, Therese. Nothing can change our relationship."

Control. Focus. Change the subject.

"I'm afraid to ask, but has Wade returned?"

"We'll be joining everyone shortly. He failed, by the way. I don't know how he pulled off the racetrack, but he failed miserably at the airport."

"Airport?" she squeaked.

"Yes. It was fun discovering just how much you and the authorities knew about the *show*. It seems there's an entire task force assigned to me." He dangled a phone between his fingers. "This is what you've wanted by the way. It has all my real contacts. Potential buyers. Sellers. Records. Secrets. You have that look about you now, Therese."

"What look?" she asked, her throat and mouth suddenly drier than dust.

"The look of desperation has settled in your eyes and caused a crease in your brow. Don't worry. I like you, darling Therese, and you've been a huge help over the years. But because of your betrayal, the end you're facing won't be quick and it definitely won't be painless. I intend for it to be long and humiliating, until you beg to join your ranger friend in death."

Long and humiliating. Beg to join…in death. The words echoed, bouncing from one side of her aching head to the other. He slid the phone back into his jacket and crossed to the door. She darted out, causing Sal to draw his weapon and Rushdan to jump in retreat.

"Sorry, sorry." She slowly reached for her boss's hand. "I trusted him and was duped just like you."

"Don't deny it, sweetheart. You helped him right into my inner circle. And I was never duped."

"When he contacted me weeks ago with his sob story, I had no reason to doubt him. Then Friday night he put it all out there to help me." She used one hand to cover her eyes and hitched her breath a little. "I don't know why I fell for it, Rushy."

"Give her the shot." His hand hesitated on the doorknob before he left. Had she made him doubt her guilt even a little?

Not a chance.

THE DIRECTIONS GIVEN to Wade on the burner phone took him north of Dallas. Straight highway gave him access to an express lane and made up some of the time he'd lost waiting on the FBI specialist to check out the computer.

With Heath's help, they'd discovered the laptop meant nothing to Reval. It was all a ruse. Something to keep him and the task force busy. *While he did what?*

Killed Therese. Sold the algorithm. Set up in a location where he couldn't legally be touched.

Wade had left the task force behind in Dallas waiting for a hint of what they needed to deploy to protect the cities in the metroplex area. The Rangers—his friends—were en route via helicopter to his destination. He still had the cloned phone from Reval and they could hear through it.

If he wasn't shot on sight and if he could get Reval to brag, then the others could relay the info to the rest of the team. They'd all agreed the plan had a lot of holes. Too many what-ifs for any of them to feel comfortable. And they'd all left the most important question unasked…would he be able to hold it together *if* Therese was dead?

He honestly didn't know. He kept telling himself not to go there. Kept repeating that he would be fine. He'd be able to do it for her. He'd finish the job she had begun. But he was also realistic.

Being there might change everything. Seeing her might…

The GPS indicated he should make a left turn, and he slowed to stop on the side of the road. The warehouse wasn't what he'd expected. Damn if it wasn't lit up like a strip mall parking lot. It wasn't old or broken down.

"Why the hell did Reval bring me out here?" He said it for the team to digest even though he couldn't hear their reply. "This place is brand spanking new. At least there seems to be a place for your chopper to land. Open parking lot, open fields around it. And completely in the middle of nowhere. See you on the other side, guys."

He turned into the lot, backing right up to the front door. *Why not?* He unlocked the gun safe built into a panel of his truck then tossed his keys in the cup holder. If they made it out of the building alive, it might help them escape.

Heading to the main door, laptop in hand, he gave it a tug and it opened. An electronic bell alerted anyone who could hear that he'd walked through the front. Security cameras followed him from the entryway down the empty hall of offices.

"Hello?" He raised the laptop over his head and shoved his shoulder into the last door.

Staying in the doorway, he searched the almost-empty warehouse.

"Walk straight ahead."

"They're waiting inside the office."

About halfway to the wall in the middle of the emptiness, the two who had spoken to him stepped from the darkness. One pointed an automatic weapon at his chest while the other frisked him, then pushed him forward again.

"Open the door and go inside."

Sure enough, the wall had a door. He hesitatingly opened it to find an exact replica of the office he'd stood in earlier that morning. Rushdan Reval sat behind his desk. Sal stood on the other side of the door. The two men from the chase the night before were on either end of a fish tank empty of fish.

Therese was on the couch. She sat with her head back as if she'd fallen asleep. She didn't stir and seemed to be out cold.

"I guess the party can get started now that I'm here." Wade held the laptop out in front of him.

The nerdy guy from the airport stepped through the door after him and took it. He opened it on the desk, punched several keys and shook his head. "Just like we thought. Bogus info. No tracker. You still want him to do it?"

"I think with the proper motivation he'll do fine." Reval waved his hand toward the unconscious Therese.

Damn.

Chapter Twenty-One

Wade's mind got stuck on what Reval had done to Therese to keep her so solidly out of commission. He shifted gears to what the criminal who'd escaped the law too many times had planned for them both. Why here in this remote part of Denton County?

"I suppose a good investigator like yourself," Reval said, leaving the comfort of his chair, "wants to know why you're needed."

"You might say that."

"Access, access, access." Reval moved toward Therese, leaning on the arm of the couch closest to her. "I need to get in and out of a place without detection."

Reval flicked his finger in the air and the nerdy man at the laptop crossed the room and held out his hand in front of Wade.

"We'll take the phone back from the racetrack."

Wade pulled it free from his back pocket and handed it over. The younger man pulled a screwdriver from his hip, popped open the cover and removed both the battery and SIM card. One of the what-ifs had just happened.

Wade was cut off from the team. They'd be deaf and blind until they landed and set up some type of surveillance.

"Tell me how much of my plans does the Homeland task force know?"

"Homeland?" Wade tried to play dumb. "I don't work too much with those characters."

Reval slapped Therese's check, snapping her head to the left, but she didn't react.

"Wrong answer, Ranger Wade. You won't get very many, so you might want to be truthful."

"You drugged her. What did you give her?"

"You see my predicament, don't you, Hamilton? You're here and I'm certain you didn't come alone. But I still have a problem." He splayed his hands toward Therese. "I need to know if her task force has discovered my plans."

"There's no reason to hurt Therese. She didn't pass anything to me."

"Oh, she's not hurting. I promise she's not hurting…yet." He pulled a syringe from his jacket pocket. "But we could make certain. Just one more little push and she won't have any pain at all ever again. That the path you want to choose?"

Reval lifted Therese's arm. He'd do it. Wade didn't have any doubts.

"Okay, okay. I believe you. But I honestly don't know what you're talking about. I followed your directions at Love Field and brought the laptop back to you."

"Then why are you so disappointingly late?" He shifted the needle closer to her vein.

"I… I had to hide until the cops searched the entire airport because of your men. I got here as soon as I could get back to my truck. What more do you want me to say?" Dammit. Even he thought he sounded like he was lying.

"Maybe we should try to wake her up?" Reval stood, backed away and slashed a fat finger through the air. Sal and his armed companion moved across the room.

"I don't know anything. Nothing." Could Reval's computer guy tell that the FBI had searched what was on the laptop?

"Don't waste my time, Wade. This isn't a negotiation," Reval continued. "Tell me what I want to know, but you're right. An overdose is such an easy way out for Therese." Another flick of his finger sent Sal and the second man to either side of Therese.

"Wait. Look, I don't know what those two inept morons you sent to Love Field told you, but I followed your instructions. I'll do whatever you need me to get done." Wade's heartbeat skyrocketed. They were going to torture Therese.

He had no way to stop it or let anyone know it was happening. And she was still out cold.

They hooked an arm under Therese's arms, semi-standing her, then dragged her to the fishless tank of water against the wall. Wade hadn't noticed that the tank stood just a little higher than waist level. Not before Therese's head lobbed forward and her long hair fell to drift in the circling water.

Therese was suspended between the two men.

"Stop! What do you want me to tell you? I wouldn't be here if the Rangers knew anything."

"Do it," Rushdan commanded.

They lifted her higher and shoved her head underwater.

"She'll drown. Are you trying to kill her?"

When Therese struggled and kicked to get air, Sal let her catch a short breath before shoving her down again.

"Come on, Reval. This is between us. If you don't believe me, then put my head underwater."

Reval nodded. Sal grabbed Therese's hair and wrenched upward. She spit out tank water as she sucked in air. She tossed her head, waking up from whatever drug Reval had given her.

Therese kicked and twisted to get free. Then they did it again.

And again.

Wade grabbed the edge of the couch and held his breath along with Therese. Each time she got close to getting a deep breath, Reval's men sent her under again.

Reval snapped his fingers and Sal grabbed a fist of her long hair, yanking her back. No one said anything as she slowly recovered.

"W... Wade?" Therese gasped.

"Reval, dammit, stop. I did what you asked. You

want the money. I'll get the money I'll have it first thing in the morning. Just don't do this to her any longer."

The men allowed Therese to collapse on the floor. Wade watched her back rise and fall as they gave her a long break to recuperate.

Reval casually walked back and forth in front of the windows that looked out to an empty warehouse. He flipped his phone between two fingers, then tapped it against his chin.

"Here's the deal, Hamilton. I don't believe you, and Therese shouldn't have, either. If she's not a dirty undercover cop—which, looking back over the past three years, I think she is. Then, she's just plain bad luck. Either way, I need to get rid of her."

"His phone," Therese whispered.

"What was that, my love?" Reval bent and grabbed her hair himself, yanking her head back to see her face.

"Every…thing on phone. Forget me."

"Well, look at that. Seems she is a cop and willing to sacrifice herself for the better good. Are you Ranger Wade? Are you going to insist that you aren't here undercover and you aren't a part of the elite task force set up to stop my show?"

Therese was lifted and shoved under the water again. Once there, her face was jerked toward Wade. Eyes wide and scared, hair swirling around her face, she was upside down, holding whatever breath she could. Then Reval snapped his fingers and Sal grinned.

Sal pushed on her harder, lifting her feet off the soaking wet carpet. She was practically to the bottom of the tank when her air escaped in a large set of bubbles. Wade wouldn't let her die. Not like that. Not because of him.

"All right! Let her up!"

"And what?"

"I'll tell you what I know. But let her breathe."

Reval waited another long second before nodding his head to bring her out of the water. Sal didn't move fast enough. Wade jumped from the couch and shoved Reval's men out of the way. He lifted Therese and laid her on the floor, immediately pushing against her belly.

"God, she's not breathing." He needed to push properly on her diaphragm and get the water out of her lungs.

Wade situated his hands, ready to begin CPR, when both men grabbed his arms. He struggled, pushing them away. He shoved on Therese's chest once, twice. They grabbed him again.

"Enough!" Reval shouted. A weapon was fired into the ceiling, causing his men to freeze. Wade was finally unrestricted and forced pressure on Therese.

Therese coughed. Water spewed from her mouth. She turned on her side, still throwing up water. Wade gave a rough shake with his body when both men grabbed him again. They released him and he gently stroked the hair away from her face and tried to reassure Therese she would be okay.

He loved her so much he'd do anything to keep her

alive. He had his answer. He chose her over everything.

"His...his phone," she struggled to say.

Wade understood. The information they needed was on the phone Rushdan Reval had in his pocket. He helped Therese sit up, his eyes falling to the burner phone left in pieces. Damn, the men of Company B wouldn't know.

Whatever happened, he and Therese were the only hope of stopping this man. Of stopping the terrorists who wanted the algorithm.

With her dying breath she'd been telling him what he needed. And with her dying breath, he'd discovered he'd tell Reval anything to keep it from being the last thing he heard her say.

"So, Ranger Wade, let's hear all about this task force the government has brought together to stop my little show."

Chapter Twenty-Two

They were waiting. At least half an hour. Maybe longer. Therese had no idea.

Rushdan's men had taken their watches and phones, locking them in this fake office. At least they had a working toilet. With Wade's help she'd even rinsed the fish and whiskey smell from her hair in the sink.

"What time was it when you arrived?"

"After ten at night." His eyes were closed as he lounged in the corner of the couch.

"I don't know how you can sleep."

"I'm not. You're doing a good job keeping me awake."

"How can you relax like that?"

Wade sat up, blinked rapidly and pushed his fingers through his hair, making it stick straight into the air. It would have been cute under different circumstances.

"Okay, I'm sitting up so you'll think I'm completely awake."

Shoot, it was cute. She quit her pacing directly in front of him. "You need to fix your hair."

"What's wrong with it?"

"Smooth it down."

He clasped her hand and tugged her to his lap. "Now you can fix it however you want."

"This isn't the time, Wade."

"Of course it is. I'm not going to fight with you, Therese. You can be mad at me, but I'm not flinching."

"I'm not mad at you. I'm..." She covered her bruised cheeks with her fingers, whispering underneath them, "Why aren't we trying to get out of here?"

"I had a good look at this box from the outside. We're covered by men with long guns and there's nothing to hide behind if we do manage to knock down one of the walls." He tugged her fingers from her face.

"Still..."

"You nearly died tonight, sweetheart. I wouldn't have... I mean..." He cleared his throat a couple of times and pulled her into his arms closer.

"I didn't die," she whispered, dropping her head to his shoulder. "How long until your partners come bursting in that door?"

"After they freak—because I'm not there to calm them down," he answered softly into her ear. "They'll find a way to discover what's going on. Then they'll wait because we're all taking our orders from your boss."

"And they're after the programmer."

"And none of them know we could get that information right now off his phone."

"Right." Reluctantly, Therese pushed back to look into Wade's eyes again.

She had no clue what he thought. After being undercover for three lonely years, she still couldn't get a read on this man. Even with time on their hands, she couldn't broach the subject of their differences. Too risky.

"I should probably..." She began to move from his lap. "You know, if they come in... Oh wait, your hair."

Wade used both hands to smooth it down.

The door opened with a grunt from Sal. "Time to go. Hands behind your backs."

They were both handcuffed and walked out the back of the warehouse. Wade had filled her in on their location and his curiosity about it. When they walked outside, why they were there was explained with one word...helicopter.

"We'll make an emergency landing at DFW. Flashing your badge around will get my men where they can have access to the systems they need. After we're done, we'll take off, leaving the two of you behind to do whatever you want."

"That's it? You think I can flash my badge and no one will call for confirmation?"

"If they try, it'll be up to you to make sure they don't." Reval climbed inside next to the pilot. "Let's speak plainly. If I don't get what I want Hamilton, neither do you."

"You'd kill her?"

"You know I will."

Sal placed duct tape over both their mouths. They climbed up and were strapped tightly in.

It wouldn't be a long flight to DFW. The control lights put off enough light for her to watch Wade's eyes move around the small bubble they sat in. She was wedged between the guy with glasses and Wade. Sal on his other side.

The helicopter bobbed up and down and around. She'd never been affected by things like this before, so it was probably the drug Rushdan had given her earlier. Her head spun and she wanted to be sick with the hopelessness consuming her.

Right up to the moment that Wade tapped on her bare foot to get her attention. Just looking in his eyes gave her strength. He gestured with his shoulder and eyes. Looking at his strap and then the pilot. This time she had no trouble discerning what he thought. He wanted to crash the helicopter.

Crash it. Stopping the potential attack. Probably killing everyone on board. She shook her head. No. They needed the programmer. Sure, one of their team members might find an extra phone on Rushdan. But the programmer would be gone as soon as he didn't get his information tonight.

Wade bent his ear to her mouth.

"Too risky," she said under the restrictive tape. "No."

The sounds from the helicopter were extremely loud without a headset, which the others were wearing. But he understood the no. Or at least she hoped he did.

Therese stretched her mouth to loosen the tape around her bottom lip and chin. Then she pulled at it by scraping the corner against Wade's shoulder. He copied her movements until they both had it free enough to talk. No one noticed the loose tape since it still connected on the top.

"Can you hear me okay?" she asked directly in his ear.

He nodded and then turned his mouth to her ear. "So we're not going down in a blaze of glory?"

She shook her head. She'd been willing to die in that fish tank, but knowingly dropping out of the sky... Maybe the drugs had clouded her mind enough then, to where she'd given up hope. But now it was different with Wade next to her.

"We can find a way through this without killing ourselves." She truly believed that.

Wade responded with a raised eyebrow and a look toward the pilot.

She used her chin to get his attention again. "I know what you're thinking," she said, continuing their dialogue directly into his ear. "But circumstances change."

He drew his eyebrows together questioningly before leaning to her. "You didn't do your mind-reading trick. I'm waiting." Then put his ear back to her lips.

Explaining what had been in her mind during the

time she'd been struggling to breathe would take longer than a helicopter ride. And maybe fewer restraints. She wanted to kiss him and tell him how glad she was to still be alive.

It didn't make sense to go there. To tell him how she felt—especially about him. Or did it? Would she get another chance?

"Okay, I'm not a mind reader. But I need to tell you how grateful I am that I found you last night. Sorry to get you involved, but once you were, I've been truly grateful not to be alone."

He nodded but didn't turn to speak.

"You know we actually met a long time ago," she continued.

The young man sitting next to her pulled a white Stetson from a gym bag at his feet.

"What the hell?" Wade shouted.

Apparently it was loud enough for everyone to hear. Rushdan's man slapped his hand across the duct tape again—first hers, then Wade's. It was the first time she'd looked at what the younger man with glasses wore. White dress shirt, slacks, Western boots and a silver star inside a circle. Wade's Texas Ranger badge.

Add the Stetson and people would assume...

So why hadn't they killed her and Wade back at the warehouse? Why did they still need them alive?

The helicopter changed directions. Fast. Then began a spiral. It was dark, but she could tell they were close to DFW. No one around her looked panicked. They were staging an emergency landing.

They would be on the ground and all have their weapons inside the airport perimeter.

Staged or not, it felt real, like an out-of-control roller coaster stuck on the same loop.

The man next to her dropped his headset, placed the Stetson on his head and then loaded a round into the chamber of his handgun.

It seemed like forever but actually only took a few seconds before they landed with a hard thud. Rushdan was out first and opened the door closest to Wade. The man dressed like a Texas Ranger ripped the tape from their mouths and unbuckled her. He tugged until she was sprawled face first on the pavement. Sal did the same with Wade.

The sound of the helicopter winding down was accompanied by the smell of smoke. Nothing was wrong mechanically. They'd just covered their tracks.

"Either of you say a word and we shoot your partner," Rushdan said.

"I would have remembered meeting you, Therese. So what are you talking about?"

She wanted to laugh at what Wade had chosen to whisper next to her. But the boot in her back kept her quiet. That and knowing Rushdan would kill Wade.

"Howdy," the fake Wade greeted the emergency crews. "Sorry for the bit of excitement."

Wade tapped his boot against her leg. "I've never said howdy in my entire life."

Chapter Twenty-Three

Wade had been pulled to his knees. If he'd wanted to tell someone what was going on, he couldn't have. There was no one to tell. Since the helicopter hadn't been on fire, the airport first responders left. Two cop cars were between him and any law enforcement officers.

Reval's plan to get into DFW Airport had worked. The pilot stayed with the helicopter. The computer guy impersonating him—something he'd make sure charges were brought about—stood guard with a handgun and a long gun. They'd done a good job separating him from Therese, who now sat in the locked back seat cage of a black-and-white.

"I'm sorry but our transport can't get here for another fifteen," Reval explained. "I wish we could get out of your way."

"No problem, Deputy," an officer said.

Cargo planes passing by on the local runway drowned out the rest. Reval shook hands and rejoined the computer nerd.

"When are they leaving?" the nerd asked. "Our window is closing."

Reval took the long gun from him, propping it on his hip. "The car with Therese is staying. Make your move after the other one departs."

"Got it."

Wade pulled at the cuffs. Whoever gave the movies the idea that it was easy to dislocate your thumb to slip handcuffs off had to have been crazy. He tried and didn't succeed.

The second unit pulled away and computer nerd removed his handgun, shifting it, ready to bring it up to take aim. He'd obviously had some type of training, and looked military calm. Wade moved slowly, trying not to be seen, shifting one foot from back to front, ready to stand.

The remaining police officer turned to face the computer nerd, who raised his weapon.

"Take cover!" Wade yelled too late.

The officer went down as Wade threw himself into the computer nerd, trying to stop him. The nerd moved but was able to recover before Wade took him to the ground.

Wade ended on his back with a gun barrel under his chin.

"Andrew, put that away and get him up," Reval said, jabbing the long gun and forcing Wade's neck to stretch.

Andrew the nerd guy pulled Wade to his feet and immediately punched him in the kidney. "You can't save anyone, Hamilton."

"Now, Andrew, you know he might be able to save Therese if he does as he's told," Reval said, pointing the gun at the police car.

Getting their attention back on himself, Wade said, "Why do you need me? Not that I'm in a hurry to leave this world, but Andrew thinks he looks pretty good in that hat."

"Make sure Andrew gets what he needs and there's a chance I'll let you both go."

"You really think I believe that?"

"I think *she* does. I don't understand how you turned her after last year. She was so loyal."

He'd let Reval think that was what happened. It would just get bloody sooner if the criminal knew Therese had been undercover this entire time.

"Let her go now and I'll give you my word."

"Your word means nothing to me. And I don't want to let her go." Reval stuck the long gun under his arm and used the nail on his little finger to pick something from between his teeth. "You can earn her freedom or she comes with me. Think about that while you help Andrew."

"At least let me say goodbye."

"No way. We need to get this over with. We've wasted too much time talking," Sal said from behind them.

"I think you might really care about our Therese." Reval used his hands once again and made a sweeping sign toward the police car. "Make it quick."

With a vocal protest heard under the engine of a

freight airliner, Andrew unlocked the back door. Therese got out, but the kid kept a hand on her shoulder.

"So this is goodbye?" she asked.

"I still think you're pulling my leg about our first meeting."

"Really? That's all you have to say?" She laughed a little even as Andrew pushed her back inside the car.

"You go first," he encouraged.

"All right… I love you. Keep yourself alive."

"You owe me an explanation," he shouted as the door slammed.

He could have said he loved her, too. The words were in his heart and on the tip of his tongue. But not like this. Maybe he should, since her admission gave him courage he didn't realize he'd been missing.

Therese placed her forehead against the window. Her long dark hair fell to either side, hiding most of her face. If she looked up…made eye contact with him… But she turned, dropping her head to the back of the seat.

THERESE'S BLOOD PUMPED through her veins, making her lightheaded. She'd said it. Admitted that she loved him in the least romantic setting ever. Captured.

She blinked rapidly to keep away the tears. Yeah, she wasn't a girl who cried. Even when the love crush of her life didn't say he loved her back. *Blink. Blink. Blink.*

There are more important things on our plate.

Like how do we get free and prevent a domestic terrorist strike. Yeah. That.

Rushdan Reval took the keys and opened the driver's door. "You both have twenty minutes. Deploy and get back to Hangar Four," Reval told Sal and the kid. "You know we won't wait for you, Andrew."

Deploy what?

"Don't worry. I could do this in my sleep," Andrew answered.

Deploy what?

The algorithm, naturally. Andrew must be the programmer. She'd already pushed and twisted the handcuffs, making her wrists raw. There was nothing in the back seat of a police vehicle to help her. She wasn't wearing anything useful—not even shoes.

Andrew shoved Wade to get him moving. To where? Too many unanswered questions. After nearly drowning, admitting that she worked with Wade and that she loved him…there was little chance Rushdan would release her.

She needed the handcuff key and had no idea even where to look. The kid Andrew had snapped the metal bracelets on her, but maybe—just maybe—Rushdan had kept the actual key on his person.

Rushdan got behind the wheel and was joined by the pilot. *Curious.* Andrew and Wade ran across the field to a group of buildings.

"Where are we going?" she asked through the police cage.

"We're leaving. For good. After this *show* there won't be a need for any more petty moneymaking schemes. My clients will know what we can do and will be paying anything I ask."

"Aren't we leaving in the helicopter?"

"Why would we do that, my dear? It's so much nicer to fly in a private jet. Especially to South America. You'll love it there."

"You aren't going to kill me?"

They didn't travel far. Across a large parking lot from the building where Wade and the kid were entering. It was too dark and too far to read the name on that building. But by looking above it as she was escorted from the car, she could see a tower.

It must be a control tower for private and cargo planes. By accessing this system, Rushdan could gain access to the main air traffic control network for DFW.

"You're going to crash planes? Are you crazy?"

"By your standards, most definitely." He yanked her along with him through a small door the pilot had already unlocked.

"Please don't do this, Rushdan. So many people could be killed."

"I won't be doing anything except living the high life in Costa Rica or Buenos Aires or the Mediterranean. I haven't really decided." He made his signature disgusting sound as he sucked his teeth open to a smile.

SHOWING THAT HE was entirely out of shape, Andrew uncuffed Wade's hands while continuing to huff, puff and curse as they ran. They waited on a security guard to open the door and then the nerd placed the white Stetson on Wade's head. It sat on the crown instead of his forehead, obviously not fitting.

"Doesn't seem to be my size."

"No one cares. You tell the guard we're here to serve this warrant." The kid pulled a piece of paper from his back pocket. "Don't worry. It looks real and is for one of their people on duty tonight."

"And what if he says no?"

Andrew fingered the handgun holstered on his hip. "Convince him or he dies now. And then your girlfriend, of course."

"You feel like a tough guy? A big shot? Shooting that cop back there is the action of a coward." He waited for his words to rile Andrew.

They apparently did, but as the kid started to unholster his weapon, the door opened. Andrew held up the fake warrant, but he remained silent.

"I'm Texas Ranger Wade Hamilton and this is my partner. We're here to serve a warrant on…"

"David Liteman." Andrew flicked the fake warrant.

"Before you object," Wade cautioned the guard and took a step inside, removing the ill-fitting hat. "We know this is a highly unusual situation. But we wouldn't have been allowed on the grounds if it wasn't all cleared. Right?"

"Somebody should have called me," the guard grumbled. "But hey, it's only my job. What do I know about protocol?" He turned his back on them and went to his desk. "Nobody ever tells me anything."

Wade entered, followed by Andrew. He could take this kid at any point. There wasn't anything tough about him. He was just plain more experienced and knew what opportunities to watch for. The kid didn't.

Point in fact, he could have disarmed the kid coming through the door.

"Is he upstairs?" Andrew asked.

"Yeah. Where did you think he worked, here at my desk? Elevator is around the corner, but if you don't want him to see you coming, the stairs are back this way." The guard pointed back over his shoulder.

Andrew walked into Wade's back. Okay, that was another place to disarm him. Throw one punch and the kid would be out cold. He steadied him, waited for him to turn around and followed him to the stairwell.

Yeah, kid, I'm following you, not the other way around.

Once in the stairwell, Andrew seemed to realize he was vulnerable. He waited until Wade passed him and then left two stairs between them.

"What do you need access to?" Wade asked. "Are we going up to the control windows?"

"Not if there's computer access outside the room."

"Like from the supervisor?" Wade pointed to the sign just under the second-floor symbol.

"That should work."

"Where did you get the idea for this malware thing anyway? You that smart, Andrew?" Wade held the door open, hat still in his hand and waited for the kid.

"I mean, you seem smart and all. But no one does stuff like that alone. Right?"

"Smart?" He waited at the top step. "I take exception to that description. I opened your sealed court records in less than a minute. This algorithm took me years to develop. The sophistication of the decryption capability is insane."

"You developed it all by yourself? That's hard to believe."

Andrew pulled his handgun. "Oh no, you don't." He waved the barrel, indicating Wade should go through the door first. "Why do you want to know about me?"

"Hey kid, I have no clue about computer viruses. Nothing like that. None of it's my cup of coffee." He shrugged, taking a step into the second-floor hallway.

"Coffee? It's your cup of *tea*, you ignorant cowboy." Andrew relaxed his direction with the gun, dropping the barrel toward the floor.

Just another opportunity for someone of Wade's experience. And now that he knew Andrew was the programmer...

Wade tossed the Stetson to the kid, whose natural reaction was to catch it. Then Wade grabbed the kid's arm and used his momentum to flip the gun backward behind Andrew. He turned, pinning him to the open stairwell door, lifted his elbow hard into the man's chin and heard the gun drop to the floor.

Then for good measure, Wade pounded his fist twice into the kid's solar plexus, knocking his breath from him. He dropped him facedown to the floor. Out cold. Wade rolled the kid over, grabbed hold of his collar and slid him across the slick linoleum floor to the elevator.

"But I don't drink tea."

He frisked the kid, looking for a phone. Nothing except a flash drive, which he pocketed. He pulled Andrew onto the elevator. He hated doing it, but if was going to save Therese, leaving this guy with the incompetent guard was his only option.

"What the hell is going on? Did he fall?"

The guard stood and moved while Wade jerked on the kid, sliding him through the elevator doors. He'd seen an empty office on the way to the stairs, which would be a good place to lock this terrorist up.

"Look, I don't have time to explain. Call 911 and get this man to a secure—"

"Help me," Andrew whimpered.

Wade couldn't finish the sentence. Words and thought left him as something slammed into the side of his head. He hadn't seen it coming. Nothing.

Chapter Twenty-Four

Damn blind spot floated through Wade's mind as he rolled in pain. Blurred vision. Pain. Cool floor against his skin. More pain.

"Yeah, this is Randy Allister in the northwest tower. I need help. I ain't kidding. This is the real thing."

Wade used his arms in an attempt to push himself to an upright position. It didn't work.

"Tell 'em not to come in hot. A woman's life depends on it," Wade said. But he didn't know if the guard listened to him.

Randy Allister seemed to be dancing around the room, gun drawn in one hand, radio in the other. Wade managed to roll over and the guard seemed to move faster or maybe there were two of him. He lifted his hands, trying to calm the inexperienced guard down.

"Listen to me, please." Wade covered his left eye, eliminating the double vision. "Randy, I've got to get to Hangar Four."

"You ain't going anywhere, man. I brought you down, imposter."

"You brought down an authentic Texas Ranger. But I'll forget all that if you just let me get to Hangar Four."

"No way. Capturing you might save my job."

"You mean because you let us in the building to begin with."

"Yeah, well. They'll forget that part when I show 'em I captured you."

Wade rubbed the side of his head, vision clearing a little. "I doubt that. You're letting the real bad guys get away."

"Don't listen to him," Andrew screamed, trying to get up and away from Wade.

"Tell you what, Randy. We'll both sit here in your custody if you just get on the horn and ask the cops to check out Hangar Four." If Wade couldn't get to Therese, maybe other cops could.

"No! You can't!" shouted Andrew. "He's...he's trying to trick you. I watched him shoot one of you in cold blood. He's still lying out there."

Wade used his heels to slowly push himself to the wall next to the desk during Andrew's yelling. He didn't want to injure the guard, but he had to get to Therese.

"You can both stay right where you are until the DFW cops get here. They can decide which of you is lying and which is telling the truth."

"Listen, Randy. What would it hurt to ask your friends not to flash their lights on the way here? I'll wait." He stuck his hands behind his head. "I won't give you any trouble."

"He's right, Randy," Andrew moved to the same position. "Be the hero and save this woman's life. She'll die if the terrorists see the cops."

"Terrorists? What kind of terrorists? Is something going to blow up?" Randy began nervously shifting back and forth, mumbling the word *terrorist* with each step. His movements and chanting made Wade's headache grow exponentially.

"Just get on your radio and call it in."

"No! Don't listen to him," Andrew shouted, drawing Randy's attention. "They'll kill her."

Wade took advantage of the moment and pulled his jeans leg up over the boot with the Love Field guard's weapon. He'd grown used to the weight and almost forgotten it was there until feeling it while lying next to Therese earlier.

If he was lucky, neither the guard nor Andrew would see him remove the handgun. Not that his luck had been holding during the past two days.

The radio squawked and Wade used the distraction to pull the gun. Andrew jumped up, sliding feet first, using the guard's ankles like second base. He popped back to a standing position gun in hand.

Wade stood covering his bad eye to search for the radio.

Andrew roared, dipped his head and charged. He crashed into Wade. The force took both of them rolling into a watercooler stand but they both managed to hold on to their guns.

Back on the floor, they were at a standoff, pointing the guns at each other.

"Find your radio, Randy!" Wade shouted, keeping his gun on Andrew. Then told the kid who pointed the gun at the guard, "Don't do it. Put it down."

The guard crawled on all fours. Andrew's barrel vacillated between Wade's head and the back of the guard.

"Got it!" Randy raised the radio in the air.

The reverb of the shot rang in Wade's ears as he saw the poor guard spinning to the side from the force of the bullet. Wade pulled the trigger. He couldn't allow Andrew to fire again.

Wade's aim was true.

Andrew's eyes were wide and fixed, staring at him as if he didn't understand what had happened.

"Oh my God. I've been shot. I've been shot," Randy kept chanting.

Wade stood and removed the gun from Andrew's death grip. He went to the guard's side, taking the man's free hand and placing it on the wound.

"Keep pressure on it like that. Good. I'm sure someone heard the shot and will be downstairs to help you."

"Are you guys really terrorists?" Randy asked.

Wade grabbed the radio and turned for the door. "He was." He stopped and pulled his badge from Andrew's belt. "This is mine."

He pushed the door open with his shoulder. "This is Texas Ranger Wade Hamilton. Cars approaching northwest DFW, refrain from lights and sirens.

Possible terrorist with hostage at Hangar Four. Be aware am on foot and armed. Ambulance needed at tower. Officer down. I repeat, officer down. Don't run code."

"Hamilton, stand down. Team is on the way," a voice he recognized told him. Recognized as one of the men making decisions about this operation. But Steve Woods had no clue what was actually going on.

Wade dropped the radio and covered his bad eye to limit the double vision. He couldn't be sure which hangar was number four, but directly across the concrete lot—large enough for two 747s to pass—sat an empty police car.

He had to get to her. So he ran.

THERESE PROPPED HERSELF on an old desk in the corner of the cramped hangar. The airplane took up most of the room. Rushdan and the pilot hadn't threatened her since she'd gotten inside.

They also hadn't seen her pick up a paper clip before she parked herself here. While she fiddled with the handcuffs behind her back, she watched the clock above the door click off the seconds toward twenty minutes.

Maybe they'd forget about her. She wished.

"What happens if the kid can't get it done?" the pilot asked while removing the blocks from in front of the wheels of the plane.

"He'll do it. This is his crowning achievement. He'll get it done or die trying." Rushdan leaned against the plane's stairs.

"That's what I'm afraid of. The kid is a bit trigger-happy."

"He does get a bit…excited."

"It's getting close to time. We going to wait?"

"No. I have what I need. Tested or not, my copy of the algorithm will bring me millions." He laughed. "I told him twenty minutes. If we wait longer, the authorities might find his mistake near the helicopter. Go ahead and open the doors. Let's get in the air."

The pilot pushed a button and the doors began to creak open.

"And don't forget Therese," Rushdan added before climbing the steps.

The pilot waved his hand at her like he was directing traffic. It was her signal to join them on the plane. She stared at him.

"Move it."

"You don't have to do this. There's no reason to take me with you."

"The boss wants you around, so you're going. Now get up the stairs and buckle in."

"Kind of hard to do with the handcuffs." She popped off the corner of the desk and turned around to show him.

"Nice try. It'll give the boss a reason to get close. Come on." He gave her a hard push toward the plane.

The metal rungs of the ladder hurt her bare feet and keeping her balance wasn't easy without her hands. But she stepped inside the small plane, climbing into the seat closest to the door.

God, she hated feeling helpless. Or maybe it was

hopeless. She'd had her fair share of pity parties, but she'd never felt as alone and lost as at this moment. If they took off…

The pilot crawled in behind her, then into the seat to fly.

"Is this it?"

"What do you mean, my dear?" Rushdan answered as if it were any ordinary day. He moved past her to the front.

"You're just going to fly away, taking me along for the ride? Why?"

"I have patiently waited for you to come around, Therese. I hate that you allowed yourself to be taken in by the ranger. I guess he fits every girl's idea of a dream man, doesn't he. I can see why you liked him, so I'll forgive you."

"Forgive me?"

"You're mine now. You belong to me. Wherever I go, you go." He moved from the front of the plane, stopping at the seat opposite her.

"You're crazy," she whispered. And then a little louder, "I don't *belong* to anyone. Especially you."

"I disagree. Once we get to South America, you'll be dependent on me for everything. Water, food, clothes, protection. You'll be grateful then."

"I'll never be grateful, you sicko. Who would be grateful to their kidnapper?"

A loud noise from outside the plane got their attention.

"That must be Sal or Andrew. Looks like you'll have company back here after all."

Body slams, crashes and sounds of a fight grew louder as Therese searched out the windows of both sides of the plane. It had to be Wade. More thuds and metallic slams—someone being thrown into the hangar door.

"Sal? Andrew? What's going on?" Rushdan yelled.

"Pull up the steps, boss. We gotta get out of here," the pilot yelled from up front.

Therese Ortis's family had not raised a helpless girl. She'd never be a woman who was dependent on any man's whim. Especially this terrible, sick man. Her eyes met Rushdan's across the aisle, then darted to the staircase.

The plane rolled forward, leaving the brightness of the hangar, only the dim lights from the controls illuminating the cabin. Rushdan reached for her seat belt. Therese scooted forward in her seat, blocking his hands.

This is going to hurt.

Chapter Twenty-Five

The plane taxied forward from the hangar. Wade had run across the giant parking lot. He was about to pull the door open when someone slammed into him. He hadn't seen anything out his bad eye.

Sal was all over him. Wade kicked out, shoving the crazy man off. Sal turned, jumping on him, forcing the gun from his hand. They both fell to the cement floor and rolled, only stopping when they hit the metal hangar wall.

Wade landed on top and got in the first punch. Sal no longer had a smirk on his face to wipe off. He shoved with both hands and Wade's injured head banged against the wall. Hard. Wade thrust the pain aside and threw his weight into pinning the bigger man down.

The plane kept moving. He could see Reval through the doorway as it passed. Could see Therese through the window.

Sal freed himself by rolling. He wanted on that plane.

"Not so fast." Wade jerked on his legs. Sal kicked

out, keeping Wade a leg length away, then rolled and twisted to his feet.

The man's eyes were narrow slits as he used the back of his hand to remove the blood dropping from the smirky tilt to his mouth.

"You want a rematch? Come on. I'll teach you a thing or two." Sal gestured for Wade to come at him. Taunting.

Wade didn't want to engage. He needed to stop that plane from taking off. He needed to save Therese's life. But this man was in his way.

His fingers curled into fists. Then he relaxed, steadied his breathing, found his center and waited for Sal to advance.

"You think you can beat me?" Sal danced from side to side like they had all the time in the world.

Wade kept his good eye focused on his opponent. He watched for the first kick and deflected it with one of his own. He followed with two punches that connected with the center of Sal's chest. Sal absorbed some of the momentum when he took steps backward but quickly charged.

Wade received a right cross that he hadn't seen coming. It stunned him enough that he staggered, giving Sal time to run to the back corner of the hangar.

RUSHDAN MUST HAVE seen the direction of her gaze and made a move to restrain her. She stood slightly, shoving her shoulder into the fat man, keeping him off balance. She took a step forward and he fell back to the seat he'd been occupying.

She stepped over his sprawled legs and leaned against the doorway. She'd nearly fallen trying to step up. How would she get down now that the plane was on the move?

Worrying about how to get down the gangway was a bit bizarre. She had no way to grip anything, with her hands cuffed behind her back. The plane would only gain in speed. She had to go now.

Two men fought at the edge of light from the hangar. She recognized Wade as he swung, connected with the other man's ribs, spinning him sideways. But the other man countered by slamming the back of Wade's thigh, forcing his knee to the ground.

"Therese," Wade shouted between defensive grunts. "Get out of the plane! Now!"

The other man—Sal—removed something shiny from his waist.

"He has a knife!" she shouted to warn Wade.

It was ridiculous to wait for a better opportunity. Each second seemed to flash by. A huff behind her let her know Rushdan was on the move. She took the first two steps. Then the madman was at the door, trying to grab her.

Sal suddenly soared away from Wade, running to catch up with the plane. Therese took another step down. Sal's arm stretched toward the ramp.

One more step. Just one more step. She had to jump. Before she could, her body lurched in reverse, her back falling across the steps. Rushdan jerked her hair, pulling while she screamed.

Having completed its turn, the plane revved its engine and sped up. Therese had no way to hang on. The handcuffs on her wrists were caught on the metal rungs as she twisted, trying to get free. She tugged and pulled her hair from Rushdan's grasp.

The plane sped up a fraction more and she lost her regained footing. She slid free, slamming to the concrete, taking Sal with her.

He landed an arm's length away. In the time it took for her to get her bearings, he straddled her and had the knife raised.

The knife descended while she rolled to her side, trying to deflect the blade from her chest as much as possible. Pain. Her own hiss and scream blocked out all the other sound.

Then a deep shout of pure rage echoed around her. Sal took it as a warning, jumped up and pulled the knife. Coming out was worse than going in. She screamed again, twisting in pain, blinking away the wetness in her eyes.

"You okay?" Wade asked, his hands gently cupping her face. "You're bleeding. Bad."

"Catch him," she gritted through her teeth.

"I think the help can take care of him," Wade knelt next to her. "I need something to put pressure on the wound. Now, don't think I'm trying to be sexy." He joked as he took off his shirt and stuffed it between her arm and ribs.

Each time she opened her eyes, she could see the

flashing lights of the emergency vehicles. She had to convince Wade to go after Rushdan. "I'm fine. Go. They don't know him," she got out after a groan. "He's crazy."

"The plane's surrounded, sweetheart. He's not going anywhere. Dammit, No one can see us. I need help getting these cuffs off."

"He has a copy of the algorithm." She squeezed her hands into fists, trying to control the stinging pain. "You've got to find it."

"Stay conscious, Therese. You need to tell me when we supposedly met."

WADE RAN AFTER the plane to get help. It was the only reason he left Therese lying alone in front of the hangar. He caught up with the cars that had brought it to a halt and caught his breath on the hood.

"My partner. She's bleeding. Need ambulance." He pointed behind him. "The man…armed with a knife somewhere around that building."

"You Hamilton with the Rangers?"

He nodded. "Yes. Can you take me back? Got a handcuff key and med kit?"

"Your team is almost here."

"I can't wait, man. Get her an ambulance."

"Hello out there," Rushdan called from the plane. "We'll surrender, but only to Ranger Hamilton."

"Aw, hell."

Therese needed him. Rushdan Reval was crazy. She'd said it. He agreed. What could he possibly accomplish by going to that plane and taking the man into custody?

He might be able to save lives. And if he didn't try, he was totally sure about one thing... Therese would never forgive him.

He pulled the DFW police officer in close. "You take this car and find my partner. You get her to the hospital no matter what she says. Got it?"

"Yes, sir."

"I need your restraints and your weapon."

"Ranger Hamilton?" Reval shouted.

"I can't—"

"Yes!" Wade nearly grabbed the officer by his shirt front, but dipped his head and regained control. "Please. I'm trusting you with her life."

The officer moved and moved quickly, handing Wade what he needed and jumping in his car. He pulled away like the plane was about to blow.

Oh, damn. What if the plane was rigged to blow?

Chapter Twenty-Six

Wade stuffed the gun down the back of his pants and slapped together the Velcro of the protective vest the officer had shoved at him. He walked with his hands raised toward the stairs of the plane.

"I'm here. You can come out and surrender. Pull off your jacket, hands on your head so we can see you're unarmed."

"Wade, I can't say it's good to see you alive. Come on in."

"Not gonna happen," Jack said from Wade's right side.

"I guarantee you that ain't happening," Slate said from his left.

Heath nodded from his position, pointing a long gun at the nose of the plane. The pilot cut the engine and placed his hands on his head.

"Time to join the party, Reval!" Wade called out. He had to focus on getting Reval out of the plane and finding the second copy of the algorithm. Get this done. But his real attention was on the ambulance that had pulled next to the police car at Hangar Four.

If he could just finish this, he could center his attention on Therese.

"You are surrounded," a voice called through a bullhorn. "Come to the door with your hands on your head."

Wade took a step forward. Jack and Slate pulled him back.

"Don't, Wade," one of them said.

Wade's mind was with Therese. He looked at the blood on his hands. The man in the plane had caused all this.

"If she dies…" he ground out in anger, marching forward before his fellow Rangers could stop him. "Get out here, you filthy coward."

He stopped at the bottom of the stairway, one hand on the rope that would have pulled them closed, one foot on the bottom rung. Rushdan Reval appeared in the doorway, hands in the air and no longer smiling.

"Get out."

"I'm on my way. Don't let them shoot me." Reval took his time, handling the steps carefully.

A lot more carefully than Therese had been able to manage. If she hadn't fallen onto Sal, she might just have a few scrapes and bruises instead of a deep knife wound.

Wade jerked him from the last step, spun him around and raised his fist. "If anyone was going to shoot you, it would have been me."

"Whoa, buddy," Jack said, blocking Wade's right hand. "I'll take it from here. You go see about your girl."

Jack placed the restraints around Reval's wrists. Then turned him, searching his pockets, pulling the shoulders of his jacket down to limit his movements more.

"Where is it?" Wade shouted.

"What?" all the men asked, including Reval.

"He has a copy of the algorithm. Therese said it was on the plane. And there's a second phone with all his terrorist contacts. He had it on his person before we left in the chopper. So where is it?" Wade demanded of Reval. Dammit, he wanted to leave.

Jack found a phone but not a second. Wade remembered Therese's dying declaration that they needed the phone.

"We'll take it from here." Steve Woods, Therese's handler, stepped forward to take Reval off his hands.

"He's been using a second phone. It's probably hidden somewhere on that plane. I wouldn't trust anyone else to look for it if I were you."

"You're right," Steve answered, handing off their domestic terrorist to another ranger. Then he slapped Wade on the back. "Great job. I'll meet you at the hospital."

"She lost a lot of blood. The officer said they're moving her to Baylor Grapevine. We cleared to go?" Heath asked behind them.

His friends stared at him and he stared at Therese across the parking lot as they strapped her to the gurney. Jack's hand came down on one shoulder, Heath's on the other.

"She'll make it," one of them said.

Wade couldn't speak. He was willing her to beat the odds and survive. She had to live. They were a good team. She thought so, right?

The ambulance doors shut. God, he could only assume she was still alive, because they were rushing away. Lights flashing, sirens loud and fierce.

The idea that she might die hit him. His knees buckled. If his friends hadn't been on either side of him, he would have fallen to the ground.

He fought the emotion to keep it from his voice, "Get me out of here."

"Sure, man. We got a car waiting."

They walked him to a vehicle. At some point during the ride to the hospital, one of them peeled the vest off him and handed him a T-shirt. Major Clements met them at the emergency entrance and told him the tower security guard was fine. He'd be reprimanded, but he would live.

"She's going to be okay, Wade," Clements said.

Sometime in his haze and daze, he began believing they'd both be fine. Even if the eye injury kept him from working as a ranger in the field, things would be great if Therese was with him.

God, he really was in love. They barely knew anything about each other, but they knew enough. She was definitely the woman for him.

Therese would live. He deserved some good luck. They both did.

"It's ABOUT TIME you woke up, sleepyhead." Wade's face filled Therese's vision.

"I think that's the first sound sleep I've had in years. Painful but sound. What time is it?"

They were both alive. Wade raised a straw to her lips and she took a long sip. The cool water felt almost as good as his skin next to hers. It was just his arm, but she used her hand to rub it comfortingly.

"You should ask what day. It's been two." Wade scratched his chin covered in stubble. "You're going to be okay. Sal missed everything vital."

"Doesn't feel like it." She tried to joke but the words sounded rough.

"I bet. But before you convince me to play that question and answer game… Or before the nurse comes in here and they kick me out… You'll want to know what happened after you lost consciousness."

"I didn't pass out."

"I assure you that you did." He kissed her quickly on the lips and sat back down, taking her hand into his. "Reval surrendered and they caught Sal trying to climb out over the barbed wire fence of the airport. Steve searched the plane, found the phone with all the contacts and the algorithm. I had Andrew's copy. Reval swears there were only two. Homeland's priority is to verify that."

"That's good, but—"

"Turns out Andrew was the sole programmer— according to him. Something else DHS is checking into. It looks like his algorithm was just a fancy word for a highly capable decryption code that was designed and modified to take over air traffic control stations. If terrorists had gotten their hands on it, they would have brought down planes, or worse. Unfortunately, Andrew didn't make it. He fired on the tower guard and I had to shoot."

"Can we get back to what's important?"

"I can give you more details later. All you need to know is that Reval is going away for a very long time. No deals."

"I'm glad we managed to succeed with both of our goals. Now you owe me…" She couldn't believe he looked puzzled. "You don't remember our first fight? Come on. You wanted him put away. And I wanted the programmer?"

"Oh, yeah. That conversation seems like a lifetime ago. Your lifetime, to be exact."

"I wasn't going to die. Not when I finally have the chance to live," she whispered. "Speaking of which. It's your turn."

Wade's face relaxed into a smile. He knew exactly what it was his turn to say.

"And you have a story to finish. Talk about drama. You tell me we met years ago and then you promptly get abducted." He picked up her hand and kissed the back of it.

"You first," she prompted.

"Sorry. When did we meet? Did I pull you over when I was with the highway patrol and issue a ticket?"

"Actually, you pulled me out of a wrecked vehicle nine years ago. It was May 31, near San Antonio."

"Damn. You must have just been a kid. That was a

long time ago. And you knew where I lived because you were keeping tabs on me?"

"I would never," she lied.

"I bet you would, Therese Ortis. I bet you would." He leaned forward to kiss her properly on the lips, then sat again. "I wish I could remember you from back then. How come you kept it a secret? Did you have braces or something like that you didn't want me to remember?"

"I thought I'd find you here. Ranger Hamilton, you have to spend some time in your room for us to check on you," a nurse said, walking to a whiteboard to write.

"But Debbie, she just woke up," Wade whined dramatically and winked at Therese.

"Oh my goodness, you are awake. Fantastic. I'll page your doctor as soon as I get your vitals." The nurse wrapped a blood pressure cuff around Therese's arm but looked at Wade. "Seriously, Ranger Hamilton, they're debating if they should add restraints to your bed. You'll have to go back to your room now." She put her hands on her hips but she still didn't look very authoritative.

"Room?"

"We kept him for observation," the nurse supplied.

"I have a little concussion. Nothing's wrong."

Debbie smiled at Therese. "And yet they've kept him here for two days."

"Two days? Were you shot? You've really been here for two days?"

"Yeah, but you didn't miss anything by getting

some rest. And they're kicking me out today so I can officially sleep on your chair."

Did he really think she was more interested in the task force operation than him?

"I'll be back after the day shift does their poking and prodding." Wade stood and kissed Therese sweetly on her forehead and then her lips. "Don't go anywhere without me this time."

He smiled and left before she could get a word out.

The nurse pumped the blood pressure cuff, shaking her head. "That man is too stubborn for—"

"Oh, yeah." He stuck his head through the door opening. "I love you, too. Hell, I'll even buy a couch."

TRUE TO HIS WORD, Wade brought his cell phone with him when he returned to Therese's room. She didn't realize how touch and go it had been that first night. One day he'd tell her. But today was for celebrating that they were both alive.

"You look different," Therese said groggily when she awoke a second time.

"Yeah, the nurses thought you might like me better if I cleaned up. I told them that was impossible— for you to like me more—but they insisted."

"I think the same thing about me. I must look horrible."

"Well, I won't ever lie to you, sweetheart. The bruising is pretty bad. But I'm good with it." He ran his thumb along the line of deep purple discoloration on her shoulder. "But the nurses might be right about cleaning up. I had the guys stop by your place and get some things."

"I don't know if I'm up for that."

"Come on, honey. There are a couple of big surprises you're going to want your hair combed for." He pointed to her bag.

"Can't it wait?"

"You've got about an hour."

"Wade? What's going on?"

"I had a long talk with Agent Woods. He agreed that your undercover days are done. I mean, our pictures have been all over the news and it wouldn't really work any longer."

"And…"

"There are some very important people on their way to be with you."

Therese's eyes filled with unshed tears. "You called my family?"

"Not me, but I'll take some credit."

"He threatened a lot of people to make it happen," Steve said from the doorway. "If it's something you don't want, blame him."

"Oh, I want it," she whispered. "Thank you, Wade."

"Come on, Wade. The nurses are ready to do their thing."

Wade gently kissed a very happy Therese, reluctantly leaving her room.

He stuck his hands in his jeans pockets and wandered to a pillar to wait. Steve followed.

"Thanks for getting the Ortis family up here. It's

the best way you could have thanked her for the sacrifice she made for this country." Wade stuck out his
hand for Steve to shake.

"I heard what you said. It was the very least we
could do. I also heard your physical didn't go so
well."

"You heard right. I've got some permanent eye
damage." He dropped his head, staring at the floor.
"Looks like a spot will be opening up in Company
B."

"Are they transferring you?"

"I resigned."

"Got something in mind?"

Wade looked up at Steve. "You offering?"

"Actually, Homeland wondered if you and Therese
would be interested."

"I don't know. I just bought a couch."

Steve looked confused. "They move those along
with the other furniture."

"Honestly, I'd be happy sitting around a pool for a
while. Whatever she wants. You know? I'm not willing to give her up yet."

"I bet you aren't. Same thing happened to me a
long time ago. I made that mistake. Let her walk
away. Worst day of my life."

"But you're married now, right?"

"That I am. But this is your story and you've got
time to think about it." Steve shook his hand again
and Wade watched as the agent walked down the
hall to the exit.

The nurses came out of Therese's room, leaving

the door open. Wade's phone vibrated with a message that the family had arrived. He didn't have much time.

He knocked before entering. Therese sat up in bed, ready for visitors.

"They're on their way up," Wade told her. "It took them an extra day to get here. I think Heath told me one of your younger brothers attends Washington State."

"I know." She grinned. "I kept tabs on all the people I loved."

"So you are a stalker." He crept over to her side.

"I said you were more like a hero crush." She held her hand out, wiggling her fingers for him to take hold. Which he did.

"That does sound a lot better than stalker," he teased.

"Why don't we just keep that as our little secret." She slid her finger down his nose, landing across his lips.

"I won't ever tell. But I will be exacting blackmail on a regular basis." He leaned in for the long, extended kiss he'd wanted for days.

She wrapped her arms around him, bringing him to sit on the bed next to her, ending their kiss in each other's arms. He could have stayed there. Finally resting because she was awake. And safe.

But her family was on their way. Jack had picked them up personally. Wade sat back, wondering how he would tell her he'd had to resign. But he had a feeling she wouldn't mind. That she'd support him in whatever he decided to do.

Life after being a Texas Ranger...

"Hey, I ordered a couch."

"Really? That's what you think is important right now."

He turned off all the outward charm and stared at her. It was one of the few times in his life he actually tried to be serious. "I never had a reason to buy a couch before. This is a pretty big deal."

"Wade Hamilton, are you asking me out?"

"Well, I do have a couch we can make out on now."

Therese wrapped her arms around his neck, tugged him close and kissed him again.

"Now we have to rescue a dog."

"Oh no. No animals. This thing is plush leather. The real stuff. Not that fake pleather."

Epilogue

Six weeks later

Wade's heart pounded in his chest. It could probably be heard by the people sitting at the next table. He'd never been this nervous in his life. Time was running out to change his mind. But he didn't want to change his mind.

Nope.

He was frightened about the upcoming situation he let himself be talked into. What had he been thinking?

"Are you okay?" Therese asked, reaching around her now empty plate to grab his hand. "Should we go to the hotel instead of trying to see a late movie?"

"No. No. I'm good. Sorry. I've just been thinking."

"Well, that's obvious. I don't mind heading back if you're tired. You did drive me to Fort Worth for a lovely weekend and brought me here for a very fancy dinner." She squeezed his hand tighter. "You *are* springing for dinner, right? Did you forget your wallet?"

To answer, he drew his hand away, pulled his credit card from his wallet and held it in the air, signaling to the waiter. Therese leaned back, wiping the corner of her luscious mouth one last time with her napkin.

"I didn't need dessert anyway."

"Did you see something you wanted?" He barely got the words out when her foot connected with his. He mouthed an "ouch" but it hadn't hurt.

"No, silly. I'd love to head back, too." She winked.

The waiter came and went with the card and Wade took her hand back into his. Things were good. Great, in fact. But they needed this weekend before he headed out for Homeland training.

All their spare time had been spent together, but that had been limited. Between wrapping up the case, grand jury testimony, paperwork, applications, more interviews... Well, they'd barely seen each other. So, yeah, he got the hint about heading back to the hotel.

But first...

They walked hand in hand from the restaurant toward the hotel.

"Hey, what's up?" She dropped his hand, wrapping both around his biceps and giving him a squeeze. "Are you worried about training? They said your blind spot wouldn't be a problem in your new analyst position."

He shook his head, shrugging, and mumbled that he was fine. He could feel her disappointment as she loosened her grip, letting her hands fall to her sides.

Damn...he could barely swallow and his knees

really felt weak. He was just nervous. He hated to admit it, but if he wasn't careful he would blow all the elaborate plans.

Maybe he should tell her and not find out if she enjoyed surprises. He'd been assured by his best friends' girlfriends, Vivian, Kendall and Megan, that *all* women liked this kind of surprise.

Wade scooped up Therese's hand, raising her arm above her head and forcing her into a twirl in the middle of the sidewalk. She laughed. He did it again until they were both smiling and he could forget his nerves.

A minute later they were there.

Sundance Square.

The fountains glowed with a gold light. He'd been told by Megan, Vivian and Kendall it was the perfect backdrop. Beautiful. Great for pictures. Something they all said was important. New traditions and all that.

Tradition?

He'd never had much of that but wanted it now. Even if Therese hadn't mentioned it. Not once. A sign the major and Fred had both warned him of.

Their friends were all around them. He recognized the men from their hats and the women who ducked behind them. But the one woman he loved hadn't noticed. Or at least she didn't give him any indication she had.

Too enthralled with the kids running through the plaza fountain, she didn't seem to pay attention to anything behind them. She was focused only on walking and being happy. Maybe on seeing the show she'd mentioned or just getting back to their hotel.

He wanted to scoop up Therese and run with her over his shoulder back to the truck. What if she said no? God, what if she said yes?

Before he could confuse himself any further, he dropped down to one knee. Strangers pointed. Mothers pulled their kids from splashing through the fountain. And Therese turned around to stare at him, covering her mouth with her fingers.

"Wade? Are you—"

"Why's everyone looking like that? Can't a guy scratch his leg?" He pulled up his dress jeans and reached inside his best boot. That was a clue for all of their friends to get a little closer. Her family sat just a little behind and Therese hadn't noticed them yet.

Therese released a long breath and spun away from him. He snagged the ring tucked safely inside his sock and worked it onto his little finger before pulling his pants leg over his boot.

He didn't move even as she took a couple of steps away from him.

"Oh, thank God. I thought you were going to pro—"

He stayed put, his arm outstretched with an engagement ring on display to everyone except the one it was intended for. When the woman with a kid in her arms pointed in his direction Therese stopped, hesitatingly turning back toward him.

Her beautiful eyes were huge, and the tips of her fingers covered her lips, which were open and in the shape of an O. She stared into his eyes, then at the ring, then back again. Her unblinking orbs filled with tears, making them sparkle.

"Is this a bad idea? Do I need to put this back in my boot?"

He spoke as softly as he could. If she was going to say no, he didn't need all of Fort Worth along with their family and friends hearing.

"Therese?"

She blinked and the tears swiftly slid down her cheeks.

Crying. She was crying. Of all the scenarios that had played through his head...*this* wasn't one of them. He began shifting, preparing to get to his feet.

He wanted to wipe her tears away, but he was stuck kneeling and quickly feeling like an idiot. All the doubts his friends had talked him out of after buying the ring slammed into him again.

"Wait!" Her hands extended to keep him where he was. "If there's a question in there somewhere... I might have an answer."

Hadn't he asked?

"Damn. Therese Ortis, would you marry me?"

"When you put it like that, how could a girl say no?" She smiled and offered him her hand.

He slipped the ring onto the appropriate finger and got up off his knee. He barely kissed her before his friends were slapping him on the back and welcoming Therese to the fold.

She began crying again when she saw her family along with Fred and his wife. Everyone was there for the important moment. Wade had never felt blessed before, but he did now.

"You had all of us worried there for a minute," Jack said.

"I was totally caught off guard." Therese smiled at Wade again.

He was still recovering from her answer and couldn't really think straight to reply. He could only feel and this...*this* was completely right. No doubts. He hugged Therese and spun around.

"I love you," he whispered into her ear. "You're not alone in life. I'll always have your back."

"I love you, too. You're the best partner I've ever had."

"I'm the only partner you've ever had. And for this—" he kissed her finger with the diamond "—the only partner you'll ever need."

* * * * *

Don't miss the previous books in USA TODAY *bestselling author Angi Morgan's miniseries, Texas Brothers of Company B:*

Ranger Protector
Ranger Defender
Ranger Guardian

Available now from Harlequin Intrigue!

COMING NEXT MONTH FROM

H HARLEQUIN

INTRIGUE

Available March 17, 2020

#1917 48 HOUR LOCKDOWN
Tactical Crime Division • by Carla Cassidy
When TCD special agent and hostage negotiator Evan Duran learns his ex, Annalise Taylor, and her students are being held hostage, he immediately rushes to the scene. They'll need to work together in order to keep everyone safe, but can they resolve the situation before it escalates further?

#1918 LEFT TO DIE
A Badge of Honor Mystery • by Rita Herron
When Jane Doe finds herself stranded in a shelter during a blizzard, all she knows is that she has suffered a head injury and ranger Fletch Maverick saved her. Can they discover the truth about Jane's past before an unseen enemy returns to finish what he started?

#1919 WHAT SHE DID
Rushing Creek Crime Spree • by Barb Han
Someone is terrorizing Chelsea McGregor and her daughter, and Texas rancher Nate Kent is the only person who can help Chelsea figure out who is after her. But can she trust an outsider to keep her family safe?

#1920 COVERT COMPLICATION
A Badlands Cops Novel • by Nicole Helm
Nina Oaks tried to forget Agent Cody Wyatt, but her old feelings come flooding back the moment she sees his face again. Now she's in danger—and so is Cody's daughter. He'll do anything to protect them both, even if that means confronting the most dangerous men in the Badlands.

#1921 HOSTILE PURSUIT
A Hard Core Justice Thriller • by Juno Rushdan
In twenty-four hours, marshal Nick McKenna's informant, Lori Carpenter, will testify against a powerful drug cartel. Nick has kept her safe for an entire year, but now, with a team of cold-blooded assassins closing in, he'll have to put it all on the line for his irresistible witness.

#1922 TARGET ON HER BACK
by Julie Miller
After discovering her boss has been murdered, Professor Gigi Brennan becomes the killer's next target. Her best chance at survival is Detective Hudson Kramer. Together, can they figure out who's terrorizing her...before their dreams of a shared future are over before they've even begun?

YOU CAN FIND MORE INFORMATION ON UPCOMING HARLEQUIN TITLES, FREE EXCERPTS AND MORE AT HARLEQUIN.COM.

HICNM0320

SPECIAL EXCERPT FROM

⊕ HARLEQUIN

INTRIGUE

*The Tactical Crime Division—TCD—is a
specialized unit of the FBI.
They handle the toughest cases in remote locations.
A school invasion turned lockdown becomes personal
for hostage negotiator agent Evan Duran in*
48 Hour Lockdown
by New York Times *bestselling author Carla Cassidy.*

Annalise's heart beat so fast her stomach churned with nausea and an icy chill filled her veins. Bert was dead? The security guard with the great smile who loved to tell silly jokes was gone? And what two women had been killed? Who had been in the office at the time of this... this attack?

What were these killers doing here? What did they want?

The sound of distant sirens pierced the air. The big man cursed loudly.

"We were supposed to get in and out of here before the cops showed up," the tall, thin man said with barely suppressed desperation in his voice.

"Too late for that now," the big man replied. He turned and pointed his gun at Annalise. She stiffened. Was he going to kill her, as well? Was he going to shoot her right now? Kill the girls? She put her arms around her students and tried to pull them all behind her.

More sirens whirred and whooped, coming closer and closer.

"Don't move," he snarled at them. He took the butt of his gun and busted out one of the windows. The sound of the shattering glass followed by a rapid burst of gunfire out the window made her realize just how dangerous this situation was.

The police were outside. She and her students were inside with murderous gunmen, and she couldn't imagine how this all was going to end.

Don't miss
48 Hour Lockdown *by Carla Cassidy,*
available March 2020 wherever
Harlequin Intrigue books and ebooks are sold.

Harlequin.com

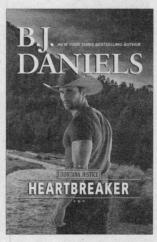